CUPID'S HEART

RETURN TO CUPID, TEXAS #6

SYLVIA MCDANIEL

VIRTUAL BOOKSELLER. LLC

One wants an everlasting love while the other only believes in the moment....

Preacher's daughter Chloe Kilian's luck with men has been less than inspirational. One was a cheater, two thought they were God's gift to women, three had Mother Separation anxiety, and four had been chosen by her father. None of the odds were in her favor of meeting Mr. Right. Ready to flee Cupid, Texas to save her sanity, Chloe decides to give love one more chance.

Attorney Drew Lawrence grudging agrees to fulfill an impulsive bet he made – one he is sure he will regret if he gets caught! A cynic, he doesn't believe in true love, happily ever after, or the town's silly Cupid superstition. The last thing he expects when he runs naked around the town statue to settle a wager is to bump into the preacher's daughter!

Drew never thought a woman could intrigue him enough to think of happily-ever-after. Will Cupid's arrow pierce Drew and Chloe's hearts and build a lasting love, or will the two skeptics, both running from the truth of their emotional wounds, be more than even Cupid can heal?

To my Critique Partners of over 25 years!
Carol Rose
Kathy Shaw
We were a great team!

Contemporary Romance
Return to Cupid, Texas
Cupid Stupid
Cupid Scores
Cupid's Dance
Cupid Help Me!
Cupid Cures
Cupid's Heart
Cupid Santa
Cupid Second Chance
Return to Cupid Box Set Books 1-3

Contemporary Romance
My Sister's Boyfriend
The Wanted Bride
The Reluctant Santa
The Relationship Coach
Secrets, Lies, & Online Dating

Bride, Texas Multi-Author Series
The Unlucky Bride

The Langley Legacy
Collin's Challenge

Short Sexy Reads
Racy Reunions Series
Paying For the Past
Her Christmas Lie
Cupid's Revenge
Science/Fiction Paranormal
The Magic Mirror Series
Touch of Decadence

Touch of Deceit

Also By Sylvia McDaniel

Western Historicals
A Hero's Heart
Ace's Bride
Second Chance Cowboy
Ethan

American Brides
Katie: Bride of Virginia

The Burnett Brides Series
The Rancher Takes A Bride
The Outlaw Takes A Bride
The Marshal Takes A Bride
The Christmas Bride
Boxed Set

Lipstick and Lead Series
Desperate
Deadly
Dangerous
Daring
Determined
Deceived

Scandalous Suffragettes of the West
Abigail
Bella
Callie – Coming Soon
Faith
Mistletoe Scandal

Southern Historical Romance
A Scarlet Bride

The Cuvier Women
Wronged
Betrayed
Beguiled
Boxed Set

Want to learn about my new releases before anyone else? Sign up for my New Book Alert and receive a free book.

CHAPTER 1

*D*rew Lawrence knew his day of reckoning had come. No longer could he avoid doing the Cupid Stupid dance all because he joined in with his brothers and agreed to the bet. But he never dreamed they would lose and the idea of dancing naked around the statue to meet love was ridiculous.

Who believed this crazy superstition.

Now, here he stood in the town square, in the buff, waiting for the church clock to strike midnight, waiting to fulfill his part of the wager he made with his future brother-in-law and childhood friend, Cody. Thank goodness, a park surrounded the God of Love, giving cover from the main street in Cupid, Texas.

"Are you ready?" his friend asked.

"I'm naked, aren't I?" Drew replied, his hands over his privates. The weather had warmed enough, he didn't have to worry about frostbite, but still, this was certifiable. As an attorney, the penalties of being caught were high.

"Remember, three laps around chanting, 'Oh Cupid statue, find me my true love.'"

"Really?" he asked, looking at his friend. "You believe this sculpture brought you and my sister together?"

"Scout's honor," Cody said.

No one could have been better for Kelsey than Cody, but he'd been told tales about the statue for years and still didn't accept a boy in a diaper managed to shoot your heart with love. Frankly, he didn't want the emotion.

"Jim and Kyle warned me you left them without clothing. Are you going to steal my stuff?" Drew asked.

A grin spread across Cody's face. "Nah, it wouldn't work a second time."

"Well, just in case. I'm prepared." Holding up his hand, he displayed his readiness. "Car keys in hand and a pair of jeans and a shirt await me inside my car. Cell phone in the car. Remember, I'm a lawyer who tries to think of all the angles."

Drew had his older brother on standby ready to race to the rescue.

"I didn't force you to make the bet. The way I recall, you guys didn't believe your little sister would fall for me."

With a shake of his head, he turned to Cody. "Like my brothers, I'm going to keep my part of the wager. Three laps and I'm out of here. To make certain the sheriff is busy, Mrs. Raffensperger's cat is once again fighting in the alley."

"Good, he'll be occupied." Cody glanced at his watch as the bells began to chime. "Time to go."

Growling at the absurdness of this humiliation because that's all it was, he took off, a ball cap covering his junk, his keys in the other hand.

"Oh, Cupid statue find me my true love, so I can put my clothes back on," Drew said, laughing.

With a sputter, the lights that normally lit up the sculpture went dark. That was odd. Drew continued running, hoping to get this over.

During his second lap, a rustling noise caused him to glance back over his shoulder as he came around the corner and slammed into a body. A female body with breasts smashed against his chest, his head snapped around.

Startled, he recognized Chloe Kilian, the preacher's daughter. "What the hell?"

"Oh no," she screeched trying to hide all her very nice curves that she obviously had kept hidden away all these years.

"What are you doing here?" he asked stunned.

With her arm across her nipples and her hand over her privates, she glared at him. "The same thing you're doing."

Chloe would believe he was running to find a lover, not to pay off a gamble. And if the superstition could possibly be true, she would be his love. That thought had him laughing out loud.

He was the last person in town who needed to do the Cupid dance. Women were drawn to him like fish to a worm. Hook, line, and sinker.

"This is not funny," she said with a hiss.

Just then he heard Cody's voice louder than normal. "Good evening, Officer Ryan. What brings you out tonight?"

"Someone called in a fake problem with Mrs. Raffensperger's cat. That pussy lost all nine lives a week ago. So, someone must be trying to keep me occupied while they dance around Cupid. Whose clothes are those?"

Drew cursed quietly. Ryan Jones, the sheriff, stood on the other side of that sculptured granite waiting to arrest whoever came around.

Even in the darkness, he saw Chloe's eyes widen with fright as she identified the sheriff's voice. Grabbing her by the arm, he mouthed the words. "Come on, let's get out of here."

Cody's stall tactics wouldn't work for long, they had to run barefoot through the wooded area.

She didn't resist as he pulled her along. They ran through the bushes, picking up scratches. Drew prayed there were no teenagers necking with their girlfriend on the swings, something he experienced as a young man learning about sexual desire.

3

Nothing like two au naturel people streaking by to startle a kid and scar him for life.

"Where are we going," she gasped.

"If we go around the park, we'll come out close to my car."

"My clothes?"

"Forget the garments," he said. "At least for now."

Running behind him, he couldn't see much of her in the shadows which was a damn disappointment after what he witnessed near the God of Love.

The preacher's daughter's curves would be like driving a Corvette on a mountain switchback - full and exciting, rounded and dangerous.

CHLOE'S HEART pounded in her chest as she gasped for breath, her long blonde hair blew in her face and she pushed it out of the way. Why in the hell had she succumbed to her curiosity and done the Cupid dance?

Because finding love was like going safari hunting for a Lycaon pictus or African wild dog. Hard to find and capable of taking you down.

They ran through the trees in the plaza, and she dreaded coming out into the light. Oh, she definitely enjoyed watching his buttocks twitch as they sprinted, but still, facing him in the darkness was one thing, but in the glow of lights, frightening. This time she should have listened to her father.

Again, if she had taken his advice, she would have wed a man so self-righteous, a therapist's couch would be a permanent fixture in their marriage. This was her last attempt at finding love and happily ever after.

"Stop," she said, breathing hard.

"We're almost to the car. Ryan could be coming behind us," Drew said halting beside her. "I have a set of clothes in the car."

"Including panties and bra?" Maybe she shouldn't have asked that question. Knowing his reputation, he probably had several sets readily available.

She knew exactly who ran alongside her. Attorney Drew Lawrence drove a red convertible sports car, usually with a hot looking blonde or brunette sitting next to him. Heart breaker, womanizer, ladies' man. Just the type of male she seemed to attract.

According to the legend, the Cupid statue thought she should fall in love with him. Who needed that kind of bitterness and despair?

"Sorry, you're out of luck there. Besides, how would I know what size you wore."

"How big a jock strap do you need?"

He turned and the shadows revealed his grin. "Big, really big."

Shaking her head, she thought this night could not become any worse. Naked, her clothes lay on a bench where the sheriff waited and she was running through the park with the town of Cupid's bad boy. What next?

"Oh good..."

"Shh!" Drew said, pulling her down behind a bush.

Two young teenagers walked along a path. They stopped to suck face and Chloe had the most incredible desire to jump up and spook them, but they'd call the cops and orange was not a good color on her, especially looking between metal bars.

Still, two eighteen-year-olds were getting more affection than she'd experienced in forever. Not since Austin, and that had been over a year ago. Right now, that just angered her.

Finally, the teens strolled on, hand in hand, and she wanted to shriek at them - 'get a room or better yet, an education before you take a test drive.'

"Come on," Drew said. "I can see the car."

As he stepped out from behind the shrubs, the sheriff's car pulled into the circle, shining its spotlight in a wide sweep. With a yelp, he yanked her to the ground, covering her with his masculine body.

Her nipples tightened and blood pulsed through her, leaving a blaze of heat as she gazed into his eyes. Skin to skin, they touched. Her breasts to his chest, his penis against her leg as the light panned over the top of the shrub they hid behind. A strong desire to push him off and run almost overwhelmed her.

Staring into his eyes, she felt his heart beat against her bosom, and she realized he was scared as well.

On top of one another lying on the grass and dirt, she felt some kind of bug crawling up her ankle, maybe a huge spider or poisonous snake.

She opened her mouth to shriek. His lips came down on hers, his mouth locking the scream inside. The urge to pound her fists against his back roiled through her, and yet, he tasted nice. Not nice enough to stop her from fighting him off to reach the creepy crawly.

Bringing her knee up, she hit him in the groin and he rolled off her groaning. "Why did you do that," he said with a moan.

"Sorry, there is a bug creeping up my calf and I couldn't shake it off," she said, slapping her skin, hoping it wasn't poisonous and she hadn't been bitten.

"You were going to scream and give our location away."

Of course, he was right, but in the moment, her imagination had that creepy crawler making its way to her private areas.

"Let me think about this. Death versus humiliation. At this point in my life, humiliation wins out, since I'm already having that experience now."

Sitting up, he glanced around and then gingerly stood. "Now that you knocked my balls into next week, let's go. From here, I don't see a patrol car. We've got a few minutes before he comes back around."

"If you brought your loud red sports car, he's probably waiting beside it for us to emerge from the park."

The car was not inconspicuous and everyone in town recognized the sex mobile.

"You like my Ferrari." A deep throaty laugh resounded from him. "Come on. Give me credit. I'm a little smarter than you think. Tonight, I drove my brother's car."

"Yes, I'm questioning your intelligence. After all, you were doing the Cupid Stupid dance," she said.

"Look who's talking. We're in this together. Let's get out of here."

Who was she to argue? At least in his car there was clothing. There she'd figure out some way to return home. Thank goodness, she rode her bike to the park and locked it so no one could steal her transportation. But her house keys...lay on the bench.

Yet, her blood pulsed through her veins at a rapid clip and she didn't know if it was from their situation or the kiss. That kiss reminded her why she chose to dance around the God of Love. And who was her forever after love?

Drew Lawrence.

A groan escaped her. No, just no. It couldn't be true. Surely the statue had made a mistake.

DREW GLANCED at the woman sitting beside him, wearing his shirt, jealous of the soft cotton caressing her breasts. While lying on top of her, he quickly deduced the preacher's daughter had a nice set of curves, firm and full and very delightful. If she hadn't kneed him, they might be doing the nasty even now.

The park had been his boudoir of choice twice before. Once in high school and then again in college. The girl from Delta Gamma, when the urge struck, wanted sex right then and right now. And at that time in his life, he'd been more than happy to oblige.

Glancing at Chloe, he wondered about the person she'd

become. The memory of her in school came back to him, and yet, she was different. Way more beautiful, but harder as well. As if her walls could insulate herself from him.

At his law firm, he was the best at reading potential jurors for a sexual assault or a divorce trial. No doubt, she would be one of his picks for the jury. Clearly, a woman who knew her rules and followed them to the letter. Good farm stock is what his grandmother would have said. So why was she here tonight?

"Who was that man talking to the sheriff?"

"That was Cody Graham," he said.

"Do you think he saw me?" she asked, a worried expression on her face."

"Don't know and I'm not going back to ask." Knowing his friend, he'd probably been sitting back, watching and laughing that the preacher's daughter and Drew were on a collision course.

He knew Cody must have seen Chloe at some point. She was coming from his direction. And the turd not saying anything before Drew bumped into her didn't make him happy.

"No," she said, biting her lip.

Suddenly it dawned on him, she had no keys, no cell phone, nothing. "Are you going to be able to get into your house?"

"Of course, I'm quite capable of breaking and entering," she said.

"You're always welcome to stay at my place," he said with a grin.

"Thanks for the offer. Sleeping over at your house. Every girl's dream for Drew Lawrence to ruin her reputation."

What could he say? So he was known as a man who liked women. Why wouldn't he? Beautiful and so easily manipulated, women adored him until they learned he never intended to marry. Even after doing the Cupid Stupid dance.

"Since I'm staying at the Cupid Inn Love Nest Bed and Breakfast, I hardly think Mabel Underwood would let me bring in women. And most especially not the preacher's daughter."

"You'd have a hard time sneaking someone past that lady," she said with a laugh.

They drove along in silence.

"Thank you for rescuing me. The ladies in my father's congregation would rip me to shreds for dancing around the Cupid sculpture. Particularly, since they're trying to rid the city of the statue."

"Why?" he asked, wondering why anyone would want to destroy the town's history.

With a shake of her golden curls, her brows raised as she glared at him, indignation flashing in her deep blue eyes. "To protect their children. They are prevailing on my father to force the town council to remove Cupid so their kids will never be tempted to dance in the town square in the buff."

"I know Ryan, the sheriff, would like it gone, but everyone else thinks it has magical powers," Drew said, remembering how Cody and his sister insisted the God of Love brought them together. Even his brothers Jim and Kyle were happy, either in wedded bliss or preparing a wedding because of their dance.

Gazing at the scantily clad woman, he realized that according to the legend, she would be his love, but he didn't believe in legends or superstitions. Facts were what he relied on, and it took a lot more than seeing an unclothed lady to make him give up his bachelor ways and settle on just one woman.

The preacher's daughter was not exactly who he imagined himself with. Maybe a model or an actress or a rich socialite.

"Stop here," she said. "This is my place."

"Do you need help?"

She laughed. "You've been gone a long time, Drew. For two years, I've remodeled houses. I'm capable of finding a way into a house."

"Just wanted to make sure you had a place to spend the night."

"I'm fine." With a toss of her blonde hair, she stared at him. "How many times have you lifted a hammer?"

"I defend the people who commit breaking and entering and find themselves looking between metal bars. So, if you need someone to bail you out of jail, I'm the man you call."

"I'll keep that in mind. In the meantime, with my background, could this be our secret?"

He shrugged. "Tonight I'll consider as attorney client privilege and no one needs to know about what occurred while we danced around the fountain."

If this became public knowledge, they would both suffer consequences he didn't want to explore. Nothing like having the whole town up in arms against him because they believed he'd taken advantage of Chloe.

"Thanks," she said. "Guess I better go. I'll get your shirt back to you."

Nodding, he gave her his best seductive smile. "We'll always have Cupid."

"Oh yes," she said, getting out of the car, a flash of her long silky legs tempting him. "By the way, nice junk."

Laughing, he replied. "Right back at you. Great tits and ass."

And they were. All she had to do was say the word and they would be sharing more than a naked dance around Cupid.

With a slam of the car door, he sadly concluded the evening was over as he watched her make her way up the drive.

Like a gentleman, he waited until the lights came on in the back of the house before he drove off. With more curves than a mountain highway, Chloe Kilian came with a lot of expectations and he wasn't a man who did well with assumptions.

Especially ones that featured a wedding ring.

CHAPTER 2

The next morning at church, Chloe walked past the group of mothers trying to persuade people to sign the petition to remove the Cupid statue. Their opposition was one of the many reasons she decided the time had come to take a chance on the superstition and learn if she could meet someone and fall in love.

Only that completely backfired and she'd run into the one man in town she never would have considered as a potential mate. Last night's adventure left her filled with mixed emotions. Disappointment in who she met, fear of getting caught, and humor at the serious lawyer whose snappy one liners kept her on her toes.

She blushed as she remembered his last words. No, she shouldn't have said *nice junk*, but her curiosity overcame her inhibitions. Everything had been out there in the open for anyone to see.

Her experience with men's genitalia was from textbooks and last night she ogled his member curious as to what one looked like. From her limited perspective, his was not extraordinary, but wasn't bad.

Tossing her blonde hair over her shoulder, she was heading to the parking lot when she froze in her tracks, her breath catching, her heart racing. Drew Lawrence strode toward her in that determined stride of his that screamed confidence. What was he doing here?

A tantalizing smile crossed his face as he reached her inside the vestibule. "Good morning, sunshine. You look lovely today, though I did enjoy what you were wearing last night."

A trickle of alarm started at the base of her spine and traveled upward causing her lungs to seize. A frown drew her brows together. Oh my, she hoped he hadn't come here to rat her out. That would certainly create a stir among the members.

"Why are you here?"

"Why else, coming to church," he said indignant. "Listening to the word of God."

"Why? You've never been here before."

The man must have an ulterior motive and she prayed it didn't involve blackmail.

"I just moved back to town. My family attended this church many years ago, before my mother's death."

That was true. The recollection of his mother and all his brothers and sister attending when they were all innocent kids returned. Before her own mother passed away.

"Okay," she said, wondering at his real purpose for being here. "Welcome to the congregation."

"Thanks," he said. "Do you need a ride home? I'd be happy to take you."

Gazing at him. "On Sunday, I dine with my father. It's kind of a tradition."

"Won't he question why you can't drive?"

A frown gathered between her eyes. The thought had occurred to her, but she didn't want to admit to her father why she didn't have her car. "This morning I walked to church. But I also have a spare key to my car."

"It's raining outside."

She glanced out and sure enough a steady stream of rain came down.

"Well, rats!"

"If you need me to, I can take you home."

With a glance, she noticed the moms against cupid watching the two of them. At the memory of what she and Drew had done the night before, she wondered what the ladies would think of the two of them dancing naked around the statue. The image brought a smile to her face.

"Usually my father and I go out to lunch on Sunday."

Out of the corner of her eye, she saw her father walking up to the two of them. Reaching out, he shook Drew's hand, but she saw the telltale frown on his face and the glint of warning in his gaze. Drew would never be on the *please date my daughter* list of eligible suitors. And her father would never approve of her chatting alone to the known womanizer in town.

"Good to see you, Drew."

"Thank you, Reverend Kilian. I'm back in Cupid to stay," he said.

"Then we'll be looking forward to having you in church," he replied, taking Chloe by the arm. "Are you ready?"

"Yes," she said. "Nice to talk to you."

He smiled at her. "Hope I run into you again."

What could she say? She knew exactly what he was referring to and it had nothing to do with seeing him in church. The man's wicked streak ran like a river and according to the legend, he was her true love.

WHEN THEY ARRIVED at the restaurant, Chloe hurried inside out of the rain. The only sit-down eating place in town, the eatery on Sunday after church was always a busy time.

"Reverend," Judy Holloway called, strolling to her father. Chloe put on her best fake smile while cringing internally. The woman chased her father faster than a hooker on crack. Like the position of pastor's wife was a job application, she sidled up next to Chloe's father.

"Happy Sunday," her father said.

"The ladies and I would like to know if you would ask the members to sign the petition to remove the Cupid statue. We're still at least two hundred names short."

"Of course," her father said.

Turning to her, Chloe's insides chilled like an artic front passing through. She didn't like this woman. Never had. And she realized before she ever opened her mouth, Holloway's question and no one would like her response.

"Chloe, I was hoping you could take the petition into your Sunday morning class and ask everyone to get behind us."

Why did people assume your opinion was the same as theirs about things like religion, politics, and even personal choices? Wouldn't you find out their beliefs before you asked them to do a task like this.

"Judy, I restore historical homes and I'm a fan of historical events. That statue was placed in the city square by the founding father of our town. While you may not like the superstition attached to the boy in a diaper, the legend is part of the town's heritage. I can't condone removing our past."

The woman's eyes widened and she stared at Chloe like an extra head had grown from her skull, spouting evil.

"Our teenagers are stripping off their clothes and exposing themselves to one another as they dance around the statue."

"Maybe their parents need to have more control over them. Though, I have to say the human body was created by our Lord and Savior and we shouldn't be ashamed of what he's given us."

Her father cleared his throat, which was his signal she'd gone too far. "I'll mention it again next Sunday and we'll put it in the newsletter. This should be each member's decision. We don't want our children doing harmful things that lead them into a life of sin."

Judy gave her a look that said Chloe owned a one-way ticket straight to hell.

After the woman walked away, her father sighed. "As my daughter, you should learn the art of diplomacy."

"So, I should lie and tell her I'll get her signatures when all I would do is throw them in the trash."

There was no way she would help this group of frightened women who feared their children might partake in the Cupid superstition. Several of the mothers probably danced around Cupid in their past. From first-hand experience, she knew it didn't work. It was a silly story that would get you into trouble. But she would not help them take down the God of Love.

"No, you just say, I'm sorry, but I don't want the statue removed. Leave it at that."

"You're right, but sometimes I enjoy watching the reaction when I say something they consider outrageous."

What would her father think if he knew about her Cupid dance? Growing up in the church, she was watched for any little indiscretion. After her mother died, Chloe suddenly had an army of women determined she would grow up correctly.

Which only made her rebel, but in her own private way. After college, she donned a pair of jeans, picked up a hammer and went to work restoring rundown houses. The love of transforming something downfallen into a beautiful living space gave her joy.

"My biggest fear has been you would decide to dance without your clothing around Cupid and get caught. The telephone would ring in the middle of the night and the sheriff would tell me my daughter has been arrested for public nudity."

Chloe had just taken a sip of water and she choked, her heart pounding loudly in her chest. What could she say? Your nightmare almost came true last night.

"If I thought the Cupid superstition would find me love, I'd do it in a heartbeat, especially with my luck with men."

Immediately, her father shook his head. "That's listening to the devil. That tale is not real."

Getting a reminder of who she met while she did the Cupid dance, she had to agree with her father.

"You can say that again," she said, not meeting his eyes. "Right now, I don't know where to meet good men."

"You've certainly dated some weird ones." Reaching across the table, he patted her hand. "My wish for you is to find the love and happiness your mother and I had. The only reason I asked those men to date you is that I prayed one of them would spark with you. That the two of you would fall in love."

"Stop," she said, holding up her hand. "It's not working, and in fact, it only pisses me off. I'm not attracted to the men you found."

"Shame Austin turned out to be such a cad. Associate pastor of my own church, dating my daughter and having an affair with a married woman."

For a moment, her chest clenched at the pain of the memory of walking into his office and seeing him creating *coitus inter-ruptus* with a woman from their church family. How stupid and arrogant did you have to be to have sex in the church? While he was diddling a member of the congregation, he and she were talking rings.

Telling her father about Austin's affair had been difficult, but she felt blessed she learned of it before she walked down the aisle and promised him forever. Before they announced their engagement.

Still, it hurt.

"Let's see, Austin cheated. Bill and Tanner believed I should be grateful to be going out with them. George, Joe, and Griffith III, had mother separation anxiety and lastly, Tom, Rick, Henry, and Chuck, you set up on blind dates. Four God-fearing, church-going, men who wanted me to give up what I love, obey them, and walk ten steps behind them."

A grimace crossed her father's face. "You're exaggerating, as usual."

"Oh, really? Would you like to see a text I received from Tom?" Pulling out her phone, she read, "Dear Chloe, being a preacher's daughter I thought you would be relieved at my offer of marriage. Be willing to sell your business and become my wife. I'm praying you come to your senses and realize you need a Godly man to take care of you, Tom."

Somewhere between when her mother and father dated and now, men had changed, or maybe she lived a sheltered life protected from the ugliness in the world. At this moment, her dating scorecard sucked. Chloe zero, losers ten. Was her luck that bad or did she attract less than stellar men?

With a sigh, her father squeezed her hand. "Your mother and I were a team. We obeyed God's commandments, but we loved and respected each other. You should find someone you can experience the same kind of love with."

Right up until the day her mother died of a heart attack in her father's arms, her parents' union had been beautiful. Since then, her father and she struggled on, missing the buffer of her mother's gentle words and understanding. The glue that meshed them together into a family. Now, her presence was sorely missed.

"I want the same thing you and Mom had, but so far, I'm not finding it. Maybe I should consider moving," she said, thinking about the job opportunity she recently read about in Austin, Texas.

After reading about the company, she sent them her resume with pictures of some of her remodeled homes. The Victorian ladies, she helped make beautiful once again.

There was a house here in Cupid she tried to purchase, but had been rejected by the owner. She wanted to restore that grand old home to its former beauty, update the features inside, but maintain the elegant history of the building.

"What about that fellow you were talking to earlier?"

With a jerk her head came up and her chest constricted. "Drew Lawrence? The renowned womanizer of Cupid? Dad, like I've told you before, you have terrible taste in men."

"Maybe I'm a crotchety old man, but I don't want you moving away from me. I like having you close. People change and Drew was at church today. Maybe he's different."

It was all Chloe could do to keep from laughing out loud. What could she say?

Oh yes, Dad I bumped into him running naked around the statue last night. He's definitely reformed.

"Hardly."

"Well, I'm going to pray on this. Your mother and I always hoped you would marry a local boy and not leave Cupid. We dreamed of living next to our grandchildren."

"We have to consider I may never marry. What if I'm going to be one of those women who never finds a husband."

Shaking his head, her father said, "I'm not ready to accept that yet."

Running into Drew in the darkness, she wondered why the statue would put her with him? There was something so wrong about waiting for the right man to come along, and then he never showed up.

DREW GLANCED around the family dinner table with a sense of satisfaction he hadn't experienced in years. It was good to be home, surrounded by the people who cared and loved him. The only people missing were his mother and father.

A nagging guilt ate at him since the day his mother died from a blood clot in the brain. Nothing should have prevented him from being there at her side.

"Drew, Cody told me you did the Cupid dance," his younger sister Kelsey said with a grin. "Who was the lucky girl you met?"

For a moment he considered telling everyone, but then remembered his promise to Chloe. "Can't tell you."

"Why not," she asked.

"Top secret information."

"Awe," Shadow, his brother's fiancée, said. "That's so sweet. We know how Kyle and Tempe met and Kelsey and Cody, now it's your turn. Who is your Cupid love?"

Maybe so, but he wasn't sharing. Chloe asked him not to say anything, and he wasn't going to tell his sister or sisters-in-law.

They had finished their meal and sat around talking, drinking beer and catching up. "Sorry, I'm not saying. My family would descend on this poor girl, letting her know she's the chosen one. Me, I'm not brainwashed by the lure of the legend. Marriage is not in my future."

Laughter from the couples had him raising his brows. "I'm serious."

"We want to welcome her," Jim his oldest brother said.

Staring at his family members, he thought if he ever married, they would accept her with loving arms, but he couldn't imagine finding anyone who could meet his expectations.

"Besides, I don't believe in that tale. It's just a way to put our little town on the map and convince people to do crazy things that gets them in trouble with the law."

His brothers and Kelsey giggled.

"Now, where did I hear that before," Cody said, glancing around the table.

Drew watched his brothers not meet Cody's gaze. What were they not revealing to him? Sure, they'd met their girlfriends and fiancées recently, but he didn't believe the superstition brought them together. Circumstance just happened at the right time and place.

"Thanks for letting me borrow your car, Shadow. If Ryan had seen the Ferrari sitting outside the park, he would've had the entire force crawling all over the square. As it was, I still almost got caught. No, I'm never doing the Cupid Stupid dance again. Not even for a bet."

"You'll never have to," Kelsey said. She raised her glass. "A toast. To our new sister-in-law, whoever she may be."

The group clinked their glasses together, including Shadow who lifted her water glass. She and his brother Jim were thrilled to be expecting their first child, so alcohol was off limits for her. The wedding would happen in about three weeks and the baby would arrive in six months. The first grandchild, his first niece or nephew. Everyone could hardly wait.

"There is something else I need to tell you," he said, his tone somber.

The family stared at him, waiting. "Before I came back to Cupid, I purchased Grandmother's old house in town. My plan is to remodel the house and make it where I live and work. The downstairs will be the office, and the back of the house and upstairs will be my living quarters."

How would his siblings react to the knowledge he bought the house with the intention of turning it into his home and office?

"I love that old house," Kelsey said. "The house needs a lot of work. I thought about buying it for the boutique, but the cost was too much for me. That grand old house sits right at the edge of downtown, so it's perfect for office space. I'm happy the place is back with the family. Mother would be so pleased."

Drew's chest tightened at how his mother had loved her old homestead. His father, not so much.

Jim and Kyle nodded.

"Glad you bought Grandmother's place," Kyle said.

"That house is a wreck, right now," Jim said. "Who are you going to hire to fix it?"

Drew shrugged. "No idea."

Cody, his friend and fellow confidant about the Cupid dance smiled at him in a knowing manner.

"There's only one person you can hire," Kelsey said. "Chloe Kilian specializes in renovations of older homes. She'd be great for the job."

Cody turned his head and looked the other way, his face a dead giveaway. If the people at the table paid attention, they would be suspicious. Unable to mask his reactions, Drew understood why Cody hid his face. One look and they would realize, Chloe was who he ran into at the statue.

"Do you know Chloe?" Jim asked. "She's reverend Kilian's daughter. The most jilted woman in town."

Drew felt like someone slapped him as he stared at his brother, stunned. Chloe had been jilted? More than once? Could that be why she reacted so strongly when she realized it was him? Neither one of them discussed their reasons for doing the Cupid Stupid dance, only tried to get away from the sheriff.

Her logic for dancing was suddenly something he wanted to understand. And he intended to talk to her the next time he saw her.

"Why do you say that?" he asked Jim.

"Every man she dates rejects her. The last one created some kind of big scandal in the church."

Was this the reason Chloe danced around the statue? No wonder she appeared disappointed her companion was Drew. But he didn't believe in that nonsense and she needed to keep searching for a husband.

"What makes you think she's good at what she does?" he asked his family. "I'll consider who you guys think is the best."

"Easy," Kyle said. "Go by and ask the owners of some of the houses she's done. Gorgeous inside and out."

Why did this seem like he was being given a reason to work with Chloe? A way to get to know her better? An opportunity to explore the attraction he'd been denying. If the woman was known for being jilted, would she take a chance on him?

The thought shocked him. Chloe was completely opposite of his type, and yet, he wanted to spend more time with her.

♦

CHLOE SAT READING a magazine on historical homes when her doorbell rang. Dressed in black yoga pants, T-shirt, with her hair pulled back in a ponytail, she'd not been expecting company. Glancing at the clock, it was after seven.

Peeking out the window, she saw Drew patiently waiting at her front door. Three days had passed since they ran the Cupid statue and every day he'd been on her mind, like a low hum in the background.

Opening the door, she smiled at him. Being polite and all.

"Good evening. May I come in?"

"Sure," she said, knowing her neighbor, Mrs. McCloskey habitually stared out her window and probably was on the phone with the women in her father's congregation rallying the troops to protect her from the bad boy in town. Her telephone should start ringing any moment.

Drew stepped into her house, a sack in his hand and glanced around at her place. "Nice. Did you remodel this house?"

Someone had told him she remodeled houses. In the heat of the moment the other night, her career seemed less important than staying out of jail.

"Yes," she said. "After college, I bought and rehabed this house. My very first job. Can I get you something to drink?"

"No," he said, stepping into her kitchen and nodding.

What was he doing here? First, he showed up at church, and

now, he stood in her house while she did her best to forget about him and her disastrous run around the fountain.

"Would you like to sit?"

"Sure," he said and took a seat on her couch. "I'm sure you're wondering why I'm here."

"Curious," she replied, thinking she liked the way he defied convention with a dark shadow of hair above his lip, his eyes emerald as the mountains in spring. Handsome as sin, she appreciated why women were drawn to him. Sexiness oozed from his pores like a fine perfume.

Taking a deep breath to quiet her overactive libido, she reminded her hormones his reputation proceeded him. Yes, they shared the Cupid dance, and she was attracted to him, but she refused to become just another of Drew's exes. After all, the word ex was attached to her name more times than she cared to remember.

"Six months ago, I purchased the Perkins homestead. Originally, it belonged to my grandmother."

Instantly she perked up. The dilapidated house sat at the edge of downtown and she had coveted it for years. Just looking at it she knew, that in its day, it had been stately and beautiful and she wanted to restore the home's elegance.

"I'd grown tired of practicing law in the city, working sixty hour weeks and fighting to make partner. So, I made the decision to return to Cupid and open an office here. When my grandmother died, my father sold the house."

Sitting back, she understood his reason for returning and couldn't help but be intrigued. She loved that big old house.

"I've now seen three of the houses you've redone and I like your work. Would you take me on as a client?"

Staring at him, she felt herself getting lost in his gaze and that couldn't be healthy. If they worked together, she couldn't act upon this attraction. But again, she had no intentions of becoming involved with the bad boy of Cupid. Why would she let him have a chance at damaging her fragile heart even more?

And this house. For years, she had longed to get inside and see how she could refurbish the aging beauty. Yet Drew might be a hindrance. At the moment, her schedule could take on a new project, one she longed to do, but it would be wise to tread carefully.

"Tell me your ideas for the house."

"The front, I want to be my office, the place where I sit with clients and we discuss their issues. The back of the house, that area I want to be my living space, and upstairs the bedrooms. Two rooms downstairs should be offices. One for me and one for my secretary who I have yet to hire."

Oh, there would be women all over town vying for that position. A great paying job, a boss to drool over, and the opportunity to snag the bad boy. Who wasn't up for the hiring process.

"Why don't I meet you at the house tomorrow morning, say nine o'clock, and I'll walk the property and you can tell me what changes you want to make and I'll see if we're a good fit."

He grinned that lopsided smile that made women swoon and shed their panties. Automatically she placed her hand on her waist to keep her undies from sliding.

"Oh, I think we're an excellent fit, now we need to know if we share the same vision for the house and talk money."

"Exactly. I'll warn you, I don't compromise on structure, and if there are design elements I think will hurt the house, then I refuse to do them. These Victorian homes should strive to maintain their history, as much as possible, while serving a newer generation. Do you understand?"

Her reputation was built on quality and sound restoration. Even the bad boy in town was not going to jeopardize her skills or reputation.

"Yes, and I'll try to keep that in mind. Grandmother had beautiful wood in her home and I hope the oak hasn't been painted or rotted."

Chloe loved the dark, rich tones of hardwood in a home, so she hoped, as well. "Why has the house sat vacant for so long?"

"The people who owned it moved out of the area and kept hoping to come back. Finally, they realized the longer they waited, the more the house went to waste. So when I learned they wanted to sell, I jumped on the chance to bring the home back into the family."

"Tomorrow, we can walk through the house, talk design, and then I'll draw up plans and we can go from there."

"Sounds like a plan," he said. The easy, relaxed atmosphere changed and she sensed something else bothered him. "Are you doing all right? I mean after the Cupid dance?"

"I'm fine. Life goes on," she said, feeling let down. For some reason, she believed in the statue and the superstition and yet her emotions were no different today than the day she ran. In fact, she feared being worse off. Because now she was drawn to an athletic, completely wrong man for her. Drew Lawrence.

"My family asked me who I met after the dance and I didn't tell them. You don't need my sister and sisters-in-law hunting you down. Plus, I promised to keep it our secret. Cody is the only one who knows the truth. When the sheriff arrived, Cody picked up your clothes and mine."

Handing her the sack. "Everything is in there."

"Thanks for bringing these back to me."

"Nice underwear," he said and her cheeks flamed. He went through her things?

"Did you find anything else interesting?"

A grin spread across his face and she could almost see the naughtiness in his eyes. "No, but that brand I buy for my girl-friends all the time."

"You purchase them underwear?" she asked in shock.

"Yeah, a matching lacy bra and panty set. Most women love that gift," he said.

Shaking her head at him, she said, "I'd say you enjoy your playboy status."

"Definitely. One of the many reasons why I'm not a good match for dancing around the statue."

"Yet, I just happened to bump into you. I wanted to find the man of my dreams..."

"And I was dancing to fulfill a bet. Does seem a little unfair," he said.

"Ya think?" she responded clearly irritated. Not only was he not the person for her, everything he said proved he was a ladies' man. She didn't need another boy child who had problems.

"Tell me why they call you the most jilted woman in Cupid."

A flash of anger rushed through her and her response came out harsher than she intended. "Isn't it obvious."

And then her phone rang.

CHAPTER 3

*T*he next day, Drew watched as Chloe, tablet in hand, made notes as she walked about the house. Even now when he came in, he could hear his grandmother telling him to make certain he wiped his feet at the door before he ran across her good rug.

Then she would meet him in the kitchen usually with a fresh batch of cookies coming out of the oven. The smell of oatmeal or chocolate chip always seem to drift through this house until the day she died. This old house was filled with memories that left him aching for the past and the love he always experienced here.

A grandmother's open arms. Those hugs were the best.

"What do you think?" Drew asked, mesmerized at how Chloe appeared in a trance as she did a thorough inspection of the rooms.

"Beautiful. The bones in this house are fabulous. The history and the architecture," she said, taking pictures with her notebook and typing in notes.

"Now the house is mine and will be in the family until my time is up," he said, watching her, fascinated at how she worked.

Glancing up at him, she smiled. "Drew, that makes me respect you a lot more."

A grin spread across his face. Why did he always seem to be smiling when he spent time with Chloe? "You didn't have respect for me before?"

"Oh, I did, but not as much. When you marry, your new wife is going to love living here."

He stared at the home that meant so much to him. Odd, he didn't want a little woman to call his own, yet he wanted to own a piece of his heritage. Sure, he had a stake in the ranch, but this was his.

And the women he dated, the models, actresses, and socialites, they wouldn't want an older remodeled home on the edge of Main Street in a town the size of Cupid. No, they required a mansion in an exclusive neighborhood surrounded by other like-minded professionals with him working sixty hour weeks to pay the mortgage.

"It's doubtful there will ever be a Mrs. Drew Lawrence. The snooty women I date wouldn't want a home like this."

Gazing at him, she shook her head. "Shame. This is a house a family should fill. Gatherings in the great room around the fire-place. The kitchen bursting with warmth and laughter, sweet aromas drifting from room to room. Children being tucked into bed upstairs. This is the kind of home I hope to buy someday."

Her words caused his chest to ache. Often, he wondered why he didn't want to marry, but marriage seemed so ordinary, and controlling and pointless.

"Why haven't you married?"

Shaking her head, she halted her steps inside the dilapidated kitchen. "You know the answer to that. Last night you asked me why I'm called the most jilted woman in Cupid."

"Sorry, I don't think I handled that well. My brother recom-mended you as the house builder, he mentioned your status in Cupid. Which made me curious because of our adventure."

Halting in the middle of the kitchen, she raised her brows at him. "How long do you have for me to tell you about my dating life? My biggest and closest call to matrimony ended when I caught him in his office at church doing the horizontal rumba with a married parishioner. I've dated men who thought I should be bowing before them because they took me out. But the worst were the ones my father chose for me who clearly had not separated from their mother's tit."

He started to laugh at the image.

Blue eyes cut at him and flashed indignantly. "Not funny. In fact, it makes you question if it's you or is it them?"

"Is this the reason you danced naked around the statue?"

Tossing her hair back over her shoulder, she licked her lips, her eyes the color of Texas bluebonnets in spring darkening.

"The women of my father's congregation are trying to tear down the God of Love. I'm not sure that superstition is real or not, but I decided I'd better run soon or risk my chance of Cupid being dismantled. Right now, my dating life could use a little excitement. Not just a little excitement, it needs a lightning bolt from above."

A frown formed between his eyes as he considered what she'd gone through. "You've never fallen in love with any of these guys?"

Picking up her tablet she had laid on the counter, she glanced at him. "Didn't say that. Austin, I loved and was ready to become his wife. Sometimes I blame myself for that one. If I hadn't been so strict, we would be married. Even when I broke up with him, he kept saying he would always love me."

"Men will say anything to stop a woman from leaving."

A heavy sigh escaped from her lips and he had the most incredible urge to comfort her. Yet, that was ridiculous. They had a connection because of the Cupid statue. Now he was hiring her to be his contractor, but there was no romance there - just an attraction. Nothing more.

"What do you mean strict?"

She looked up from the notes she was making, her big blue eyes regarding him. "I'm waiting until marriage. I made him wait until we married for sex. Obviously, he found it somewhere else."

Drew stared at her in shock. Chloe Kilian was a virgin. All his alarm bells started ringing in his head and his blood rushed to his groin in a mad dash.

Why did that seem like a challenge, and yet, he promised himself when he moved back to Cupid, he would save his hound dog ways for when he was in Dallas.

Drew didn't need or want the gossip associated here in town. Looking at Chloe, this beautiful woman stood untouched, a virgin, and all his hormones revved up like a drag car ready to sprint to the finish line. The idea of being her first left him hard and wanting and completely off limits.

A WEEK LATER, Chloe stood beside Drew, a paper mask covered their faces. The contracts were signed, the permits approved and the demolition was ready to begin. This afternoon, Drew would help her, while her crew finished a job, and tomorrow, the whole team would be here to start the renovation.

"Okay, let's pull the cabinets down, remove the countertops and afterwards we'll knock down that one wall and go from there. If we don't run out of time, we'll do the upstairs."

"You're going to add another full bathroom?"

"It's on the plans. Unless we hit some kind of snag, you'll have two baths on the main floor," she said.

"How did you get into this?" he asked. "Don't you think it's odd for a woman to be a contractor refurbishing houses."

"No, and I love it."

The lawyer was already sweating, and even though his muscles were toned and strong from his workouts at the gym, she could tell he was not used to working with his hands. Well, at least not with tools.

A grin crossed her face. That had been a magical semester, the first time she fell in love with Victorian ladies. "In college, I reno-vated a house in one of my classes and became hooked on refur-bishing old homes. Since then, that's all I've done. I'm fortunate it pays the bills."

For the next hour, they demolished the kitchen, pulling the cabinets off the wall and smashing the countertops.

In some ways, this was always a fun day. Getting rid of a little frustration while tearing out a kitchen or a bathroom. When all but one cupboard lay busted up all around them, they took a break.

"This is hard work," he said breathing heavily.

"The destruction is easier when the entire crew is here. They'd be finished in no time."

Drew stood leaning against the one remaining counter. Chloe jumped up and sat swinging her legs over the side, gazing around at what all they had accomplished, sipping on a bottled water.

"The other day, I explained to you why I did the Cupid dance. You said you danced to fulfill a bet but who made such a wager with you," she asked, needing to understand why he would take the risk.

Sure, men were known for being exhibitionist, but still, the risks of being caught by the law... Especially a lawyer. The judge would make an example out of any attorney brought before him.

"Obviously, you don't have brothers or male friends. Cody bet me and Jim and Kyle that if he proposed to my sister and she said yes, we had to run around the Cupid statue. If she said no, he would take us all to Las Vegas, expenses paid. What we didn't know was he and Kelsey had been dating."

"You're right, no brothers or sisters."

Unfortunately, her mother had never conceived again after her birth. Chloe had longed for siblings, but she also received more since she was the only child. Still, family would have been nice.

"The other two did their run a month ago. Jim is marrying Shadow next week and Kyle and Tempe eloped and now run the veterinary clinic together. Both of them found perfect partners after they ran around the statue."

"And you didn't," she said, knowing the superstition.

"No, I'm not searching for someone to marry. In fact, I did the dance to honor my word with Cody, nothing else."

"According to the superstition, I'm your true love," she said, thinking it sounded so awkward.

Leaning on the counter top, he turned and moved toward her. The green in his eyes had darkened to a deep hue that sent a sizzle of heat scurrying up her spine. There was something so determined in his steps that she knew--absolutely knew--his intentions.

Stopping in front of her, he pulled her down from the counter-top until her feet hit the floor. Trapped in between him and the cabinet, her pulse beat a little faster.

"Yes, according to the legend you are the love of my life. Maybe we should take a little spin before we make up our minds. Sure, we kissed the other night, but it was a way for me to shut you up. But now..." his mouth hovered over hers, her heart pounding in her chest. "We need to know before we go any further. Is there desire between us?"

His lips covered hers, teasing and tantalizing her as his tongue slipped between her lips and he pulled her tightly against him. Sure, she'd been kissed before. But never like the man wanted to consume her and she was his tasty morsel for the taking.

A heat began to build in her center unlike anything she ever felt before. The feel of his manhood pressed into her, hard and rigid. An explosion of need rocketed through her, sapping her strength and turning her legs into rubber. She feared they were going to buckle, but he held her up.

The kiss seemed to go on and on, and yet, she didn't want him to stop. For the first time in her life, she wanted more.

Suddenly the front door opened.

"Chloe?" her foreman called. "We're here early to help with the demolition."

With a shove, she pushed him back. "Crap."

Taking a step back from her, she barely had time to straighten her shirt and pull herself somewhat together.

"Ricardo, you guys made it. Why don't you take care of the bathroom upstairs and the one in the hallway. Then tomorrow we can start with the construction," she said, sounding like a marathon runner, her breathing rushed.

The foreman looked between the two of them.

"Okay, we'll get started," he said and turned to give the directions to the rest of the men.

Blushing profusely, her cheeks a flame, she turned back to Drew, feeling awkward.

He leaned in close. "Just so you recognize right up front, your kiss is very tempting, but I don't believe in that Cupid statue nonsense. And I don't intend to ever walk down the aisle."

"Great," she said and veered into his face. "Stop wasting my time."

"If that's how you want to think about it. I like to think that was a mighty fine kiss we just shared, and we'll soon share even more."

The sheer confidence about him, pissed her off. How dare he lock lips with her till the point of no return for his own perverse pleasure.

"Not hardly. I'm not sleeping with the bad boy in town who is notorious for his carousing. We took a spin around the block and it came up lacking."

As he stared at her, his head tilted. "Oh, honey, that kiss was anything but lacking. I'd say that kiss was a scorcher. Probably a ten and if your workers hadn't arrived, we would have made it to first base, at least."

"Dream on, Drew. You're not into marriage and I'm not a girl who dallies with men like you. In fact, I want everything you don't, so you'd be a waste of my time. We should get back to work."

Turning, she walked away, frustration with the male species mounting with every step.

SHORTLY AFTER THE KISS, Drew left, leaving her alone. As he walked out the front entrance, she wanted to throw something at the door, but didn't want to damage the old wooden threshold. Tears pricked her eyes and her chest clenched in pain.

Of all the arrogant men she'd ever met, he took the cake. It appeared her bad luck with men continued. Even after running around the fountain, her first meet was with a man who didn't want to settle down. Who didn't believe in the superstition, who let her know right up front he had no intention of ever marrying.

And he kissed like the devil. Never had she become lost in the power of a man's lips. The intoxication of the spell he created, she never experienced before. But he was all wrong for her.

At least, he didn't wait until she was emotionally involved to tell her he would never marry. The most frustrating thing was she believed in the legend and felt attracted to Drew. She could see herself as his wife. She could easily fall in love with him.

Picking up the sledgehammer, she slammed it against the cabinet. The breakup with Austin had been painful and if she didn't want to experience that kind of hurt, she needed to put distance between her and Drew. Time to back away and shut down this growing attraction. Nip these feelings in the bud and make their relationship strictly business.

With the second blow, the cabinet split in two and she began to pull the wood from the wall. Pulling the pieces, she saw what looked like a leather-bound object on the floor.

Dropping to her knee, she picked up the book and wiped the dust from the jacket. Pressing the button that unlatched the lock, she opened the binder and realized it was someone's diary. Flipping through the pages at the front, she saw the line for the owner's name was blank.

She wondered who it belonged to. Probably one of the Perkins girls left it behind when they moved. But it seemed older than the young girls' ages. Later, she'd skim through, looking for names, then return it.

CHAPTER 4

*D*rew glanced around at the people at the church picnic and wondered once again why he was here. This was his third Sunday at church and the first time he attended regularly since his mother's funeral.

Raised to be there every Sunday morning, he'd stopped attending after her death. Two family members dying so close together, it just wasn't fair. Then again, like he told his clients, life wasn't always fair.

Walking up behind her, the smell of a delicate flowery scent came to him as he breathed in her aroma. How could a woman who smelled so soft and appeared so feminine wield a hammer better than most men? When he looked at her, she was certainly not what he expected.

"Good morning," he said.

Chloe whirled around, her eyes narrowing at him. "Morning."

They had barely spoken since the day she told him he would be a waste of her time. And he understood her reasoning, but that didn't mean he wanted to stop pursuing her. For some reason, he longed to spend more time with her and thus why he returned to church.

"Wow, three Sundays in a row," she said. "What's bringing you back?"

The question bothered him. The first time had been after their Cupid dance, looking for her, and now, he was here again. But he would never tell her he felt drawn to her. Not yet anyway.

"The place to be on Sunday morning," he responded. "Besides this picnic is the best eating in town."

A light spring dress seemed to shimmer on her when she moved and it was a contrast from her jeans with the tool belt around her waist. This woman was such a dichotomy that intrigued him more than she should.

She shook her head at him as they walked through the food line, filling their plates.

"How's the house coming along?"

"Yesterday, the electrician redid the wiring, which I told you had to be done. Tube wiring is too dangerous and no insurance company in the world would insure you," she said. "Tomorrow the plumber will be out to replace old iron pipes and test the pressure."

Leaning in, she whispered, "Don't get any of Mrs. Burns homemade pickles. You've been warned."

"Thanks," he said, "for the heads up."

With his plate full, he followed her to a table. "Don't you sit with the other young people?"

"Oh no," she said. "Four of the men sitting at that table are exes and considered a dead zone."

A chuckle rumbled from his chest. "Is that why I feel like I'm being watched, with even a few whispers thrown in?"

"Just part of hanging with the PK kid."

How difficult it must have been to grow up, being scrutinized by the congregation and every time you got in trouble your world knew. Always being held as an example of how a child is supposed to behave.

"From the curves you carefully concealed beneath that dress, I don't think you're a child anymore," he said as a blush spread across her cheeks. That clingy scrap of silk made him want to act boldly. As he gazed at her lips, he remembered their touch, even her taste.

"Here is not the place to discuss my curves," she said in a low whisper.

"Maybe not, but you see, I know things about you these other randy bucks don't," he said, teasing her. The last time they were together, she'd been the one to make him uncomfortable and now he was enjoying his payback.

"What do you mean *randy bucks?*"

"Oh, come on, Chloe, you're beautiful, you're intelligent, you're fun, and these men are crazy for not dating you," he said, wondering why one of them had not snatched her up.

"Because I'm the preacher's kid, my personality should be wild and reckless with no regard to authority? Especially church rule?" she said.

"Strange, I haven't seen this side of you. Have you been holding back on me? This Chloe sounds like the type of woman I take out," he said.

A sarcastic laugh escaped her. "That's the problem. I'm me, not some stereotype everyone expects. Including the boring men sitting at that table. Some wanted the crazy PK kid, some wanted a religious church lady to keep them in line, and some just put me to sleep.

"Why is it so hard to find an interesting man? Someone who you can talk to about anything, who is more of a friend, and then becomes your lover."

"Maybe your expectations are too high? Most men are only interested in the physical side of things."

"Too bad," she said. "After the sexual side cools down, then all that's left is the friendship."

Drew frowned. None of his relationships lasted very long. Once the attraction cooled, he was gone. Quickly, he grew bored, like a child with an attention span of about thirty seconds. It sounded like Chloe had the same problem – she, too, became easily disinterested.

"Drew," a woman screamed. Sara Green ran to him and hugged him, pulling his face between her ample breasts. "I heard you were back in town."

"Long time," he said awkwardly, sitting at the table with Chloe while Sara gave him a head lock to her chest. "Been back for almost a month now."

As soon as she released him, he pulled back. "Drew, you bad boy. Call me and we'll get together and have some fun."

Oh yeah, he understood exactly what this girl had in mind. A tempting morsel that in the past he would've jumped at. But not now.

Sidestepping her invitation, he felt like he was walking on glass. "Great to see you, Sara."

Smiling at him like she wanted to pounce on him, she finally seemed to get the hint and walked away.

"Awkward," Chloe said. "Nothing like witnessing a booty call in action."

Holding up his hands. "There will be no response on my end," he said, knowing the old Drew would have been tempted to run after her, but he refused, determined to make a new start in his home town.

"I've never been so carefree with the opposite sex the way you are." Her blue eyes studied him and not in a good way. "You obviously feel comfortable in your own skin and don't mind sharing it."

Why the hell did he continue to hang with this woman? Why did she have the ability to make him aware of his shortcomings, yet, he enjoyed the challenge she represented. In fact, gazing at her, he speculated on how to respond without incriminating himself. All he could do was stare at her full lips and wish he could taste them once again.

"What's wrong with feeling good in my own skin? Do I think I'm handsome? You bet. Do I think I'm a man women want? Yes, it's been proven time and again. What's bad about that?"

Sapphire blue eyes flashed at him. "Nothing, but I don't want what everyone else has sampled."

That right there was the reason why he made the decision to slow things down a bit. There were only so many one-night stands a person could experience before they realized they were meaningless. That hour spent in a stranger's arms still left him lonely.

That brief moment of pleasure didn't leave him satisfied, but created a craving for something more. So, he slept with the next woman hoping to find that missing element. Hoping this time his loneliness would be satiated. This time, he would find a woman who wasn't as shallow as rainwater running down the street.

Why did Chloe seem to make him think about his weaknesses?

"Okay, Miss Prim and Proper Virgin, if you knew me before, you'd realize I'm no longer quite the gigolo. Since moving to Cupid, there has not been a single one-night stand, a steady girl-friend or even a date. These last couple of months, I concentrated on setting up my business, buying my grandmother's house and starting the remodeling. All thoughts of women were put on hold."

The glare she gave him let him know she didn't like what he called her. "Well, Mr. Gigolo, I'm proud of you not continuing your philandering ways. You'll live longer."

With a chuckle, he wanted to hear her response. "Why is that?"

"One day you'll find a woman who has a husband or boyfriend who didn't appreciate the fact you partook of their woman. Remember, Texas is a gun-toting state. All you have to do is turn on the TV and see it all the time on the news. Jealous boyfriend shoots man. Jealous husband shoots boyfriend. Jealous woman kills man."

"Well, thanks for being concerned about my safety."

Her brows rose and she gave him a look more derisive than accepting. "Always looking out for you."

"And I rescued you from the sheriff."

"We'll always have the Cupid dance," she said.

The urge to kiss her all but overwhelmed him, but he only sat there, his memory replaying how much he enjoyed kissing her. What was it he was missing? Why was he so attracted to Chloe?

The man, the lawyer, who dated beautiful models, actresses and a few rich socialites, no longer wanted that kind of woman. What had happened to him that now a blue-eyed temptress sat across from him and all he could think about was her innocence.

After their kiss, she seemed more remote and withdrawn while he wanted to experience more and she refused to even give them a chance.

CHLOE STROLLED around the picnic grounds, saying hello to many of the parishioners, especially the elderly. It wasn't that she disliked being her father's daughter and remembering her duties to the people of their church, in many ways she enjoyed the fellowship. The helping of one another.

In every congregation, there were always one or two who found fault with whatever she did. Those few made her want to toss aside all her teachings, but instead, she took a deep breath and responded kindly to them.

Over the years, she learned to keep her real thoughts to herself. Only occasionally she let them slip, especially with the troublemakers like Judy Holloway.

"Mrs. McCloskey how are you today? You look so bright in that floral shirt. It makes your eyes shine."

The older woman sat in a chair and smiled up at Chloe and took her by the hand, giving it a squeeze. The lady lived across the street from her and guarded her like a hawk.

"Thank you. Why are you talking to that Lawrence boy? That one's a hellion. It's rumored he slept with half of the girls in his high school graduating class. There's no telling how many women he's been with since he left home."

The woman always had the worst to say about everyone. It kept her questioning what she said about Chloe behind her back.

"Now, Mrs. McCloskey, he's been attending church. Whatever he's done in his past or present is none of our business. Right now, I'm working with him to refinish his grandmother's house. That old grand home is going to be beautiful once again."

The lady perked up and sat a little straighter.

"He bought Mildred's house? I knew his grandmother, God bless her soul. She was a nice woman who use to watch me and my brother when my mother was working the fields."

This was intriguing news.

"Mildred was my favorite sitter and I loved when she babysat us. His mother was a wildcat just like him." The old lady leaned in close like a confidant. "She met her husband, running naked around the Cupid statue. The one they're trying to get removed."

A chill went up Chloe's spine and she turned to see Drew walking toward her. The information slammed into her, overwhelming her with ramifications for her and Drew.

"That's interesting."

Glancing around to make certain no one could hear her, she whispered, "Stay away from that young man. A pretty girl like you can find a better man than that hound dog."

"That would be hard since we're working together," Chloe said. "I'll keep my eye on him."

"Be careful. A man like that has hands as fast as lightning. Your clothes will come off before you can object. Make sure someone is with you at all times."

"I'm not afraid of him because he would never hurt me," Chloe defended Drew. After all, the night they danced around the statue, he had the perfect opportunity to take advantage of her and he'd only kissed her to shut her up. Though, she would never tell Mrs. McCloskey.

"You're such an innocent woman and you don't need the trouble a man like him can bring. My nephew Charles Montfort III will be here next Sunday. I'll introduce you two. You should sit with us."

"Maybe," Chloe replied not wanting to confirm or deny. Then the memory of meeting her nephew once before and how she found him so boring and dull, she almost went to sleep during a church dinner. A real date would probably leave her comatose.

"In the meantime, stay away from that Lawrence boy."

"Thanks for the advice," Chloe said, feeling the urge to get away quickly from the exasperating smug woman. Did she not realize she was actually driving Chloe straight into his arms?

Chloe walked away, ready to escape the picnic and the well wishers, the women who wanted to protect her, the do-gooders and even the disbelievers. Needing time away from the people of her father's church.

"Where you going?" Drew called.

"Home. I've reached my people limit," she said quietly.

With a laugh, he took her hand. "Can I walk you home?"

"Sure, as long as you don't talk to me about who I should be dating. The bitchy side of me would breakout since I can't take much more before I lose it."

A chuckle came from him. "Mrs. McCloskey?"

"Oh yes," she said as they began to leave the park. "You're not her favorite person. Though in all fairness, she has someone all picked out for me."

"Who is it? I'll kill him," he said in a mocking voice.

Gazing at him she smiled. "Oh, you, a lawyer would go to prison for me."

Warmth filled her and she realized she liked this casual, teasing Drew way more than the pretentious attorney. Then again, sometimes she felt like Drew could be a chameleon changing into who he needed to become for that social setting.

"No penal institution. Remember, as an attorney, I've been inside a prison before, and frankly, I'll write a hundred boring wills to keep from going back. No, I would convince him of all the reasons he doesn't want you as a girlfriend."

"Mr. attorney tell me why he doesn't want me for a girl-friend?" she asked, curious to what Drew would come up with.

"No one knows, but she has a shopping addiction. Her credit cards are maxed out. Seriously, man, the woman wields her power tools in a manner you never want to experience."

Chloe laughed out loud. "Oh my, if he believes that then he wouldn't be worth my time. Obviously, I'm not a shopper since my main clothes are jeans and a T-shirt."

They walked along the sidewalk, the cool Texas spring breeze blowing her hair. Soon summer would arrive, and with it, the heat. For now, it was a beautiful day to talk beneath the trees and enjoy the sunshine.

"Mrs. McCloskey said she knew your mother and grandmother."

"Really. Mom was active in town, especially when we were in school. How did she know my grandmother?"

"She loved your grandmother, said she use to babysit her while her parents worked in the field."

Chloe longed to tell him about his mother bumping into his father as they danced around the statue. But she didn't have any evidence and she knew he would want proof.

"Your mother died not long after your father," she said. "My own mother had passed away three years earlier, and I remember your mother's service."

With a nod he said, "After dad's illness, I wanted to come home from college and help Jim run the ranch, be nearer to mom in case she needed me. Jim and Mom ganged up on me and said no. Finish my dream, become a lawyer, they said. Mother was determined all her children would graduate with a diploma. Only Jim didn't finish. When Dad became too weak to take care of things, Jim came home to take over the ranch operations."

As they walked down the street, a bird chirped, singing its song of bliss. Drew grew quiet and she could sense the sadness in him at the mention of his mother.

A shadow crossed his face. With a sigh, he said, "I should have been here when Mom died. We never had the chance to say goodbye."

"Sometimes we don't get what we want," she said, realizing how much his mother's death still hurt him. Pain reflected in his gaze and on his face and she had the most incredible urge to stop and hold him. But they continued walking.

"True, but I didn't want her to die alone. Dad's illness was lingering, but mother's stroke took her immediately. When Dad died we were all by his side. We should have been with Mom, as well. One day she was fine, and the next, she was gone," he said, kicking a rock with his shoe, sending it clattering down the sidewalk. "What about your mother?"

"My mom left me when I was in my teens. Since that time, every woman in church has claimed me as their poor orphan child."

While the ladies all had good intentions, they could never replace her own mother. Several years went by before she learned to let go of the anger at her mother leaving.

He chuckled. "I can see that."

Just like the women in the congregation thought she needed mothering, could Drew be looking for the loving embrace of his mother? In his own way, were his one-night stands an unconscious pursuit for the missing part of his life? A way to satisfy a void left from his mother's death? She had to ask him. She had to know.

"Did you ever consider your constant search for a woman is possibly your need to fill the hole after your mother died?"

The look on his face went from stunned to shock before he looked at her with disdain. His body tensed and he appeared almost affronted.

"You think I have mother issues? Should I call you Therapist Chloe now? Are you psychoanalyzing me to find out how I tick?"

Gazing at her, his eyes darkened and she cringed, not wanting to make him mad, but knowing she touched a sensitive nerve. Dealing with the death of her mother at a young age, she sought professional help to learn why she felt so much rage.

"No, but I saw this doctor on a talk show and he mentioned that sometimes when a parent dies and leaves behind children, we go searching for that feeling they gave us. That man helped me to understand why I was so angry at my mother for deserting me. Though, she had no choice, I was still hurt she left me behind when I still needed her."

Walking along in silence they reached her house. Finally, he turned to her. "Women are available to me. So, I partook of what they offered, though, part of me says we were both taking what we wanted. Having multiple sexual partners has nothing to do with my mother dying."

The attorney did not like to be surprised with emotions he never considered. At this point, he wasn't ready to accept that his pursuit for intimacy with women who were not right for him was his way of handling the loss of his mom. And he could be right. "Good to know. So, why haven't you found an everlasting love then?"

"Maybe, I didn't want one. Maybe I was enjoying the moment. Maybe I just wanted to have great sex."

Tilting her head, she stared at him. "You should enjoy the moment. Your mother and dad's moments ended way too soon. Just like my mother and dad's moments were interrupted by death. No one knows how long we have and I want to spend as much time as possible with the man I'm supposed to be with."

Not really wanting to hear his response, she turned and waved at him as she walked up the sidewalk to her cute little cottage. Drew Lawrence had never gotten over the death of his mother. Probably, in some irrational way, blamed himself for her passing.

She wished there was a way she could help him through such emotional pain. She'd think of something in the end.

LATER THAT NIGHT, curiosity got the best of Chloe. She'd spent the afternoon paying bills, preparing for the next week, and suddenly she couldn't stand it any longer. She had to know who the diary belonged to. The book lay on her desk, like a beacon calling out to her. Picking it up, she sank down in her favorite chair and pressed the clasp.

The book opened and she read the first couple of pages. The story of a young woman poured from the paper and she laughed at the antics of being a teenager in the early seventies. The same drama, the same angst of her own early years were revealed through the eyes of a mysterious girl. The same parental fights and how her mother wanted her to wear her skirts longer.

Quickly, she came to understand and even liked the girl. She was a sweet person who couldn't wait to start her life. Her plans to attend college doused when she learned there was no money.

Chloe read until she came to a passage close to the end:

Dear Diary,

Last night my friends persuaded me to try the Cupid dance. So, while they waited in the car, I stripped off my clothes and ran in my birthday suit around the Cupid statue. Scared out of my wits, I couldn't believe who I bumped into dancing naked around the statue.

Now according to the legend, he and I are true loves and yet, he is the biggest flirt, the most popular boy in school, the one known for dating a different girl every night. Why would I marry a man like him? Though he is awfully cute and he was sweet to me and promised me this would be our secret.

Then the man asked me to go out with him the next night. I'm going to find out if there is anything between us or another dead end. Regardless, I've decided to go to Fort Worth, get a job and go to school at night. Time to face reality - grow up and become an adult.

James Lawrence would not be part of my life.

Chloe realized whose diary this belonged to. Mary Beth Lawrence, Drew's mother.

Nerves trickled down her spine, sending a shiver rippling through her. Drew's parents had run into one another around the Cupid statue just like Drew and Chloe.

Could this mean she and Drew really were meant for each other, meeting the same exact way?

DREW HAD RENTED a temporary office until his new place was refurbished, not knowing how long it would take to remodel his grandmother's house. The plans Chloe had drawn up and then revised to his specifications were perfect or so he believed. Only time would tell if they would work with the house.

The bell above his door tinkled and he glanced up as Chloe's father, Reverend Kilian, walked in the door.

"Hello," Drew said, standing and greeting him as a twinge of uneasiness scurried down his spine. At the very first meeting, the man made it clear he didn't care for Drew. His reputation preceding him.

The man shook his hand and then sank down in a chair. "First off, I want to say welcome back to Cupid and I'm glad you're attending church, again."

Drew waited. Why did he get the feeling a big but was about

to be slammed down on him? One that probably would end with - stop seeing my daughter.

Putting his pen down and closing his laptop on the details of a case he was currently working, Drew gave him his undivided attention.

"Thank you," he said still not warm and fuzzy about her father being in his office. The man obviously had something on his mind.

"You've been hanging around quite a bit with Chloe," he said, gazing at him the way a father did when he didn't approve.

"Yes, I hired her to refurbish my grandmother's old house."

"Oh, the Perkins homestead," he said.

"Yes, sir." As a lawyer, he'd learned years ago, it was better to let the client confirm what they wanted and needed. So, he sat back and studied the older man, noticing the lines around his eyes and the way his hair had turned silver since Drew was in high school.

"Chloe's mother died when she was a teenager. A father can never take the place of a girl's mother. The ladies in the church have taken her under their wing, but sometimes I think she gets tired of their meddling, as she calls it. This morning, my phone rang with two of the women objecting to her being with you. Are the two of you seeing each other romantically?"

Drew smiled. Part of him wanted to say yes, just to piss the old man off. That wouldn't be good for Chloe. "Like I said, sir, we're working on my project together."

The man frowned and Drew wondered why would he seemed disappointed. Shouldn't he be relieved he wasn't pursuing Chloe?

"Do you like my daughter?"

A trickle of nerves gathered in his stomach and he hesitated, considering how truthful he should be. But again, he didn't want to lie either.

"I enjoy Chloe's company very much. She's a beautiful, intelligent woman."

49

That brought a smile to the preacher's face. "Chloe is so much like my Margaret. When I look at her I get teary eyed," he said softly, then he straightened and stared Drew in the eye. "I'm no different from any father. You want your children to be happy. To find someone to walk through life with that has her best interest at heart. To love and care for her."

The reverend lifted his hands and made a steeple with the fingers almost as if he were praying, while he stared at Drew. "Since you came home, you appear a more mature person than you were as a kid coming home from college. I've yet to witness or hear of any wild escapades. Maybe the playboy has finally decided to settle down."

With a shrug, Drew smiled, neither confirming or denying. "At this point in my life, I'm trying to build a practice."

A moment of silence ensued with Chloe's father carefully regarding him.

"Call me old fashioned, but I need to find a man for my daughter. Someone who makes her happy. You're not the first man I've approached, and the others Chloe rejected. But with you, I see her smiling and laughing and she seems to brighten around you. I'm looking for her a husband."

That was news. Why hadn't he noticed her reaction to him? She always seemed so confident, so sure of what she wanted and not willing to budge on her morals. Which was probably a good thing. Yet, there was the problem that he didn't want a ring and a vow.

Why was her father involved in his daughter's dating life?

"We've moved past the time of fathers choosing their daughter's husbands. Why are you trying to marry her off?"

Again, the man paused as if he didn't want to confide in Drew.

"My wish for my daughter is to see her happily married and settled before I die. Sadly, my time is limited. Doc says I have six months without chemotherapy and twelve with the drugs."

The reverend shrugged. "The Lord says it's my time and I'm

prepared to meet my maker. I want Chloe either engaged or married before I'm called home. The thought of her alone is terrifying."

Drew's chest clenched. How would Chloe react to losing her last remaining parent. The memory of hugging his mother that last time - when neither of them had known it would be goodbye - overwhelmed him. Oh, how he wished he could go back to that day and tell her how much he loved and appreciated her.

"Have you told Chloe?"

"No, and I'm not going to until I can't put it off any longer. My life needs to remain as normal as possible for as long as possible. My daughter should not be under pressure to find someone just to make me happy."

In some ways, Drew could understand. He was attracted to Chloe, but he didn't plan on finding forever after. "I'm honored you think I'm a worthy enough man for your daughter."

"Oh, son, don't misunderstand me. I didn't say that. If I had my way, she'd be going out with some boy from our congregation, but she's not interested in them. With you she appears different."

All the eloquent words on the tip of Drew's tongue suddenly ripped away. All his reasons for not accepting the man's offer drifted away like ashes in the wind.

"You're not my first choice, but I think you might be Chloe's choice."

Again, he battled his conscious. "What if I'm not the marrying kind?"

"Are you interested in her? If so, I want to know now and then I'll back off and let God do his work. If not, please back away. It's a dying man's desire to see his daughter at least happy with someone, if not you, I'll continue the search."

The thought of her father looking for someone else for Chloe sent a jealous spiral coiling like a snake inside Drew. He didn't want another man dating her. Yet, Drew didn't want to marry her, but he didn't want anyone else to have her either. It just didn't seem right.

Sometimes even when you knew your feelings weren't logical, they were still your emotions. And he didn't want anyone else to take Chloe out.

With sudden insight, he realized he wanted to date her.

Since arriving in town, he wanted to explore the attraction between the two of them. Quickly, she put him in his place, telling him if he wasn't looking for forever after, then not to waste her time.

Was he wasting her time? Was he wasting the precious time her father had left? Confusion roiled in his gut and he didn't know the answer, but selfishly longed to find out.

"At this point, I'm not going to promise you I will marry your daughter. I'll agree to ask her out. We'll see where this connection between us goes, but it wouldn't be fair of me to tell you I'll marry her. I'm not certain about marriage and only Chloe can make the decision even if I did ask her."

The older man smiled. "That's all I want. You'll make the attempt and God will take it from there."

Somehow Drew didn't think God had time to take off from worldly affairs to lend a hand in their dating, but if it made the reverend feel better, that was fine.

"Let me just say, I will haunt you if you take advantage of my daughter in any way. No premarital sex unless you want me making your life miserable from beyond the grave."

Well, that was certainly a nasty threat. Now, he only hoped Chloe never discovered he agreed to date her because of her father. For the first time, he could understand why she became so angry at the involvement of people from the congregation in her life, even when they were trying to watch over her.

Though her father's intentions were well intended, still, Chloe would think of this conversation as interfering. And it was.

"Are you going to tell Chloe about your illness?"

"As I said, not until I have to," he said. "When she learns about the cancer, her life will change, and I want to hold off as long as I can."

The old man was protecting his daughter, but she needed to know. "Don't wait too long."

"At the right time, I'll tell her," he responded.

"Let this meeting be our secret," Drew said, knowing she would be furious if she learned they had discussed him and her dating or that he knew about her father's sickness before she did.

"Agreed."

CHAPTER 5

*C*onfused and torn about what to do with regards to Chloe, that evening he walked down the street to the Braxton Family Restaurant for a bite to eat.

Staying at the Cupid Love Nest Bed and Breakfast, he tried to avoid Mrs. Underwood and her damn dog as much as possible. It wasn't that he didn't like animals, in fact, he adored the puppy Jim and Shadow were raising. The dog at the B&B, an obnoxious yapping little terrier, controlled the woman to the point he sat in her lap while she fed him.

A balmy spring breeze blew as he strolled to the diner. Until he moved to Dallas, he never realized how fortunate he was to grow up in a small community where everyone knew everyone else. Where kids still rode their bikes through the town square on their way to their best friend's house. And neighbors looked out for one another.

The only thing he missed from his old life was the connection with his friends. Meeting them for drinks and dinner in the evening, talking shop had always been entertaining. Usually during those meetups, he would find himself a nice little chica. But no more, or at least, not here.

Yet part of him wondered if that wild roaming, a different girl every other night was a thing of the past. Funny, he didn't miss that element of his lifestyle.

Stepping inside, he glanced around and observed the lateness of the hour. Most people had eaten, gone home, and were busy getting the children ready to bed. Having no babies of his own would be a disappointment. He liked kids and promised himself he would be a great uncle.

In the corner at a table all by herself, he saw Chloe, bent over paperwork. Her blonde hair spilled over the data she absorbed, her empty plate pushed to the side. His chest ached with the knowledge her father had imparted about his impending death. The urge to protect and shield her from the pain she would suffer overcame him.

If possible, he would spare her this hurt, but this was out of his control.

Stunned, his stomach roiled at the emotion as he walked toward her, knowing he had to see her, talk to her, be with her and even ask her out on a date.

Six months wasn't long, but maybe it would only take two or three dates and he would know for certain he was still never marrying. Then he could explain to her father.

"Do you mind if I join you?" he asked standing over her.

Like she'd been in a daze, she looked up and he almost laughed. This must be how he looked when he pulled an all nighter during finals week.

"No. I'm working on your plans now."

"What about my house? What are you changing?"

"Finalizing details like where wires should be run for the Internet, plumbing questions. A place for the washer/dryer. Tweaking things. This is actually the part I enjoy. Creating the design and putting a plan into action to make it come together."

Nodding, he beheld how much she enjoyed her job.

Engrossed in her work, she hadn't looked up until he stood next to her.

"We need to make a trip to Fort Worth and go to the store and choose your light fixtures. While we're there, we could look at flooring," she said once again making notes on the floor plans.

Looking at him, she smiled, her blue eyes dilated almost like she was excited. With a jolt, he wondered what she would look like in the throes of passion.

"What if we make a weekend of it. Drive up on Friday night. Pick out fixtures and later hit some of the art museums. A famous architect, Louis I. Kahn, has a showing at the Kimball, or we could visit the Modern Art Museum, or the Amon Carter Museum. Your choice."

A frown crossed her forehead. "Two separate hotel rooms?"

"I'd rather we stayed at my apartment - there's two bedrooms. I haven't let the lease go, because I'm still working on a case in Dallas and really don't have a home to move into."

Did she realize he was asking her out on a date? Or did she just think this was business? Though he accepted it was to his advantage for her to think this was for the house, part of him wanted her to understand, this was a bona fide date.

Staring at her, he could almost see her weighing her options in her mind and knew she was tempted. Dating her would be so much easier if he'd never told her the truth about his intentions-- about his unwillingness to marry.

Yet, after the Cupid dance, he wanted to be honest and let her know right up front his beliefs on the superstition and marriage.

Licking her lips, she smiled. "It's best to order this stuff early or it won't be here when we're ready for it. Yes, I'll go with you to Fort Worth and we can spend the night in separate rooms at your apartment."

"Good. I'll pick you up at six on Friday."

After this weekend, he'd have a clearer picture if he planned to continue dating Chloe. No woman had ever lasted much longer after spending so much time together. Usually, once they spent the night, his curiosity was abated. Normally that included three days of robust sex, but he doubted that would happen.

"Remember, this is our secret. My surrogate mothers wouldn't understand me staying the night with the bad boy of Cupid."

With a smile, he thought about her father. "Our secret."

WHEN THEY DROVE into Drew's apartment building, Chloe was surprised at the lavish style. Located in downtown Dallas close to his old office, the complex was designed for upwardly mobile younger tenants. After they parked his Ferrari in a well lit, guarded parking garage, he used a key card to enter.

As they walked in the door of his unit, the warm furnishings, fine décor, and the rich paintings stunned her. The place looked gorgeous. Dropping the stack of mail on a granite kitchen counter top he showed her around.

"Your room is right through here and you have your own bathroom," he said, showing her the guest room with its queen-size bed, dresser, and chest. Lamps graced the end tables and the place was sophisticated and well decorated.

"Which girlfriend was your interior designer?"

His brow furrowed in a frown. "Sorry to disappoint you, but my mother came up and we spent a weekend decorating my apartment."

"Sorry," she said, feeling guilty for assuming the worst. The memory of him working with his mother to put his home together must've been bittersweet.

"The first and last time she came to visit," he said. "Now I'm sure Mom would be thrilled to learn I moved back to Cupid. And she would love that I purchased her childhood home."

With a plop, he sat Chloe's overnight bag on the floor. They decided to return late Saturday afternoon to Cupid because Sunday was a busy day for Chloe and for Drew, as well.

A question that bothered her for some time popped out of her lips.

"Why aren't you living with Jim and Shadow. Don't they have plenty of room in that big old house."

"Those two are in full wedding plan mode. Kelsey is helping Shadow prepare her big day. From the B&B, I can walk to work. Once you are all settled, we'll stroll down the street to this little steakhouse I love and have dinner."

A smile flitted across her face. "That sounds nice. Let me change and we'll go."

As soon as he left the room, she quickly opened her suitcase and pulled out the little summer dress she recently bought online. Not that she was dressing up for him, but all she ever wore around him were jeans and a shirt, and on Sunday, it was a conservative outfit.

For once, she wanted to wear something a little sexier. Even if she dressed for him, tonight, the outfit was a rehearsal for a legitimate date.

Freshening up her makeup, she swiped on her lipstick and then hurried out the door.

"Wow," he said when she came out. "You look stunning."

Grinning, she did like his compliments. "So seldom do I have the opportunity to step out in a fun dress. On Sundays, my dress must be conservative or my rectory moms let me know I'm not dressing appropriately."

His eyes darkened. "Don't let them see that dress or you'll be locked up."

The man's words were like poetry oozing over her like warm oil, making her feel good about her appearance. Tonight, his attire was business casual with a sports coat thrown over his Oxford shirt and jeans. There was no doubt why women flocked to him.

She turned toward the door. "Come on, I'm starving."

"Oh, and the woman has an appetite. I like that."

"Sure, says the man who dated enough skinny models to fill the room sideways."

"Honestly, they're boring. Beautiful little dolls who eat maybe half a cup a meal and drink very little alcohol. Only positive thing I can say about them is sexist. So, I'll keep it to myself."

Smiling at him, she wondered about his life in Dallas. Since his return to Cupid, he hadn't mentioned much about his previous experiences here.

With a shake of her head, she laughed. "You are such a fast man."

"Ah, you're hurting my feelings. Recovering," he said. "I've been celibate for the last six months."

"Oh my, you must be suffering so badly," she cooed in sympathy not certain she believed him. What he didn't know was she had checked, and yes, her bedroom door had a lock. Tonight when she went to sleep, the door would be locked, just to make sure there would be no hanky panky. "I'm sure you have booty calls on speed dial."

Laughter rumbled from his chest. "Don't go there. Come on, let's go before this discussion gets me in even more trouble."

Reaching out, she took his hand. "Are we walking."

"Yes, we're a short block away."

His hand felt firm, his grip sure as they walked out of the apartment and caught the elevator going down. Exiting the building, a cool breeze blew through downtown as cabs honked and cars sped by.

At nine o'clock, the place was bustling. It would be fun to live here for about two weeks and then she would miss the quiet pace of Cupid.

Sometimes it was good to be reminded of what she loved about her small community.

Strolling into the restaurant, the maître d' greeted him. "Drew, are you back in town?"

"Just for tonight, Jean. Tomorrow we return to Cupid."

The man nodded at her. "Lovely, follow me," he said. "Your table is not occupied."

Chloe followed the man and couldn't remember the last time she had dined in such a fancy place. Linen tablecloths covered the table, dim lighting, soft music, and the ambiance was cozy. Glancing at people as they made their way through the tables, she recognized a local weatherman.

The maître d' pulled out her chair and she sank onto the cushioned seat.

"A bottle of your favorite?"

"Oh, yes," Drew said.

She glanced at him. "Why do I think you've done this before?"

No matter what happened tonight, she had to remain strong. When he asked her to go with him, she thought it was a business weekend. Over the course of the night, she'd decided it was more. So much more. A trickle of unease spiraled through her.

Uncertain if he was giving them a chance or could he be looking for an opportunity to strip her of her panties. Hopefully she would soon learn the answer.

Regardless, she was going to enjoy the evening.

"You're right." Grabbing her hand, he squeezed it, sending a rush of warmth through her. "If I didn't know better, I would think you were jealous of the women before you."

Laughter erupted from her. Just as the maître d' brought over a bottle of wine and opened it with a flourish at their table. Last, he poured some of the chardonnay into their glasses and left.

"If I had been drinking, I'd probably spewed all over the table," she said still smiling at the idea she was jealous. That wasn't possible. Oh, she was attracted to Drew, but the man only expected desert and she was champagne.

Drew made the decision not to become romantically involved

because of her beliefs. Chloe wanted forever after and refused to play his love games. "Look, I'm not jealous. I don't want to be seen and thought of as one of your many women. Someday I want to be someone's special woman."

Turning over her hand, he rubbed the inside of her palm, sending a delicious shiver through her. The man had the art of seduction down.

"There is no doubt in my mind you will be."

Taking a sip of her drink, she looked at the menu. "Okay, I'm going way out on a limb here. I'm going to be completely different from those skinny minis you date. I want a filet mignon cooked in wine and butter sauce with a baked potato and salad, and for desert, I want the bananas foster with the big flame and everything."

He laughed. "I like an appetite in a woman."

"Don't think I'm having a tablespoon of food."

Leaning toward her, he asked in a low voice, "Tell me again why we're not officially dating?"

Picking up his hand, she smiled. "It's not me. It's you. You're the one who was blatant about not wanting to marry. I'm a girl who requires a ring on it."

"Just my luck. I'm with the most beautiful girl in the restaurant and she has these standards."

Her brows drew together. "Tell me why again. I still don't understand your aversion to marriage."

His hand covered hers and she liked the texture of his skin against her own. Sometimes when he looked at her, his eyes darkened in that sensual stare that sent tremors rippling through her.

"Love is painful. It hurts when you lose someone. Over the years, I've found it's easier to let women know right up front I'm here to play and never get serious."

Nodding in understanding, thinking there was more he kept to himself, she said, "After my mother died, my father grieved for years. Father said he didn't think it was possible to ever find someone to fill the aching void left by my mother. That no one could replace her."

"My mother said almost the same about my father. She would never marry again because no one could be as good."

They sat in comfortable silence for moment while Chloe thought of everything he'd said. "Why do you think love is painful? With all the women who have paraded through your life, has there never been anyone who made you think she's the one? What about children?"

For a moment, she didn't think he would respond.

"I plan on being a great uncle," he said, gazing at her, his emerald eyes warm. "Why is love painful? When someone you love dies, it hurts. We were prepared when dad died and actually felt relieved he no longer suffered. But Mother's death was totally unexpected. And so close to Dad's. After that, I didn't want to feel anything anymore. So, I dulled my emotions by never letting myself get serious with any woman."

Part of her understood his response. Part of her thought he should accept that life and death went together. No one lived forever, but that seemed cruel. Though he talked of his mother and his fast lifestyle, she didn't think he realized how much his words revealed to her.

"You think it's better to never love, so you don't experience pain? How do you think your mother would feel about your reaction to her death?"

A deep sigh came from him. "Right now, I haven't found anyone I wanted to take a chance to experience love and pain with."

"Understand," she said, agreeing with him. "Me, neither."

A sardonic laugh came from between his lips as he gazed at her, his green eyes sad. "With regards to my mother, the first portion of her lecture would be chewing me out and reminding me of how I'm acting immorally. The second part of her diatribe would be to remind me of my dad and their happiness. The wrap up would be I should find a nice girl and settle down."

How she wished she could tell him about the diary. She already liked his mother even in death. And for her son to recognize her reaction was perfect.

Just then Chloe glanced up and a very thin, beautiful woman had stopped by their table. "Drew, you're back in town?"

"Only for the night," he said, glancing up at her, tensing.

"Is she your latest date?"

"Chloe Kilian," Chloe replied, holding out her hand. "I'm remodeling his grandmother's house in Cupid."

The woman relaxed and drew her fake claws back in. "Anna Provinski, one of his many ex-girlfriends."

"Join us," Chloe said, being friendly and knowing it made Drew uncomfortable. "Tell me all about your experience dating Drew."

She laughed. "A tragic short tale."

Drew, who had been taking a sip of water, made a spewing noise and started coughing.

"Are you all right?" Chloe asked him.

"Dying," he replied. "But don't worry about me."

Anna shook her head. "Thanks for the invite, but my date awaits me." After giving Drew an icy stare, she said, "Call me."

Drew did not respond and the skinny model quickly walked away.

"Awkward," Chloe said, grinning at the discomfort etched on Drew's face. Deliberately, she had engaged and kept the conversation light and easy until the girl accepted she was a companion of Drew's on a business dinner.

Was it a business weekend? Things were different between them.

"Somehow, I think, if you were driving a bus and I was standing in the road, you would run me down," Drew said, sitting back in his chair smiling at her. "Counselor, you did a great job of outmaneuvering the opposition."

"I've never driven a bus, you might need to worry," she said, leaning into him. "And the outmaneuver--easy."

§

WHEN THEY ARRIVED BACK at his apartment, Drew put on soft music, clicked on the fireplace, and opened a bottle of wine. Everything he always did to seal the deal and win the girl. Chloe would be no different and hopefully she'd wake up in his bed in the morning.

For a second, his conscious twinged, reminding him he promised her father no seducing his daughter. But they were here, the dinner was nice, he enjoyed her company more than he cared to admit, and well, wasn't this all leading up to how he treated all the women he dated. He seduced them.

Chloe sat on the couch, watching the fire as he walked over and handed her a glass. "More alcohol?"

"Seemed fitting. It feels good to be relaxing here in my own place again. Though, I know spring is here, I love this little fireplace."

Sinking down beside her as close as he could, he slipped his arm along the top of the sofa behind her. They watched the flames lick the fake logs and sipped their drinks.

"We can put one of these in your grandmother's house. There is that old fireplace that gas logs would be perfect for," she said.

"I agree," he said and took her wine glass out of her hand and placed it on the table. As he moved closer, she frowned at him. That move was one of his signature advances and worked every time.

"What are you doing?" she asked breathlessly, her sapphire eyes shining at him, sending trickles of desire spiraling down his spine, centering in his groin. Right where he needed those feelings.

"What I've wanted to do since you walked out of the guest room looking beautiful."

His lips came down on hers, covering her mouth, seducing her and hoping she felt the same hunger, that somehow, he held at bay all evening. Opening her lips, his tongue slipped inside, tempting and tantalizing her, making her want him as much as he wanted her.

Like an alluring morsel, he savored her lips as he gently laid her back on the couch, until she lay sprawled beneath him. While he enticed her mouth, his hand trailed down until he found her breasts. Kneading the full mound through her dress, he anticipated the moment he could remove the filmy material from her body.

Their lips came apart, her breathing ragged as he pressed against her center, letting her feel his hardened shaft, wanting her to know what she did to him.

"Chloe, let's move this to my room," he said as he placed kisses down her neck.

"No build-up, no foreplay, straight to your bed?" she inquired.

"Oh, honey, I'm going to make you so hot for me, you'll be screaming," he promised.

Her body tensed and she pushed him off.

"What a wonderful idea," she said softly, sitting up beside him.

A surge of happiness and anticipation had him eagerly standing up and pulling her. The need to get her into his bed overwhelmed him.

Placing her hand on his chest, her blue eyes scorching him with heat. "It's been a lovely evening. Tonight, you answered my question about us. You just want into my panties. Goodnight, Drew."

Before he had the opportunity to respond, she strolled to her room and shut the door, leaving him standing in his living area bewildered.

Unable to stop himself, he cursed, not believing she had walked away from his seduction. Coming home, he stepped right into the old Drew's modus operandi. Only this woman had slammed the door in his face, literally.

With a sigh, he turned off the gas logs, emptied the wine glasses in the sink and switched off the lights and went into his bedroom alone. Stunned, he couldn't fathom, she turned him down.

As he undressed, his cell phone rang. Glancing down at the number, he recognized Anna's name.

"Hello," he said. "How was your date?"

"A complete disaster. How about you?"

"Frustrating," he responded.

Anna laughed her deep voice sending a shiver down his spine. "Your builder, she doesn't sleep with you?"

"No, and I don't want to talk about her. What are you wearing?"

"Absolutely nothing. Why don't you come over and turn a bad evening into something special for both of us?"

Without hesitating, he reacted like the old Drew. "See you soon."

"Hurry," she said. "I need you."

Ending the call, he was out the door and all the way to the garage to jump in his car, just like the old days, when his conscience kicked in. Why did it seem like he was cheating on Chloe if he went to Anne's house? Because he knew exactly what Anne was offering, and he had no obligations to Chloe.

Yet, there was this bond with her. Instinctively, he understood if he went to Anne, there would be no chance in hell of ever dating Chloe.

And damn it, he wanted to date Chloe. Not because of her father, but because he was attracted to her in ways he didn't understand. She made him consider things he'd refused to think about for a long time. She made him look at his actions in a meaningful light.

Twice tonight, he'd fallen back into the old Drew's routine. Twice tonight, he realized his mistake. Maybe there was hope for him and for Chloe yet.

Yanking out his phone he dialed Anna back. "Sorry, I can't do it. I'm crazy about Chloe and I'm not cheating on her."

🐦

THE NEXT NIGHT they pulled up in front of Chloe's house exhausted. Saturday, they picked out the flooring, lighting, and other items she needed and even visited several art museums before they headed back to Cupid.

The day had been fun with no mention of the night before.

"I'll carry your suitcase in," he said as he opened her door.

"You don't need to see me to the door," she said, trying not to think of the weekend as a date. The night before, he had no idea how hard it was for her to end his kiss and walk back to her room. His kisses seemed to cause certain areas of her body to heat until near combustible levels.

But she was his builder, and he didn't want forever. And she wasn't going to be another one of his booty call girls. Obviously, the model-thin girl he'd talked to at dinner had been one of his exes and wanted to restart the romance.

Chloe couldn't help but enjoy his discomfort when she'd invited the woman to join them for dinner. She refused to be jealous of these women because they meant nothing. If the two of them were to ever be in a relationship, then she wanted nothing like what he had with them.

Shaking his head at her, he frowned. "Yes, I need to make certain you're in the house just fine. It's almost eleven, the house is dark and I'm not letting you go in by yourself."

"This is Cupid, not Dallas," she said, though secretly, she liked the fact he was concerned.

"Yes, but my mother raised me better than to let a woman go into a house alone at night. Don't you watch horror movies?"

"Not really," she said.

He carried her suitcase up the sidewalk while she found her keys. Once inside, she turned on lights and moved about the house, checking the rooms.

"Everything is fine," she said.

"Did you look in the closets and under the bed?" he asked.

Laughing, she said, "Hardly. The boogie man escaped years ago."

Walking up close to her, he wrapped his arms around her waist and pulled her to him. "This weekend I had a great time with you. Loved how you invited my old girlfriend to join us for dinner, rejected my advances, spent my money to pick out furnishings. Chloe, you definitely know how to keep things interesting and me wondering what's going to happen next."

Though he was serious, she giggled. "It was fun. I especially enjoyed the Kimball art museum. We made a start on things we need for the house. Dinner last night was fabulous. Your seduction typical."

A deep chuckled rumbled from his chest. "Now you can say you received the same treatment as all the other girls."

"That's the problem, I don't want to be just one of your women."

"And I don't want you to be." For a moment, his green eyes darkened as he stared at her. "Something you said bothered me."

"What?" she asked, wondering what would upset him.

"The meal, the way you looked that night, the wine, the fire, it felt like the perfect moment. The old Drew came out and slipped right back into his habits of seducing a woman."

A smile lifted her lips. Could they have crossed some internal barrier keeping them apart? "Yes, and he's quite the charming fellow. Now I understand why so many women fell for him."

Picking up her hands in his. "All right, I admit I wanted to get into your panties in a bad way. If you'd given me the chance, I would have taken it as far as I could've last night. For once, I agree. You were right to put a halt to things. This weekend showed me I want to be involved. I'm crazy about you and I want us to date."

"You don't want to marry," she said, her voice sincere and quiet as his hands gripped hers.

"Why can't we date and find out where this goes."

"Because I fear I'll be the one who will get hurt. You've made yourself perfectly clear about marriage and I've told you I'm looking for someone to spend forever with."

Biting his lip, he stared at her. "I understand. Give me a chance. Let's put the idea of marriage on the shelf for now and see if there is something between us. Let's have fun together and then later if we realize we're falling in love, we can then discuss what we're going to do."

A glimmer of hope filled her. "You understand there will be no premarital sex? You'll consider marriage after we date a period of time or let me know your views are the same?"

When she stared into his emerald gaze, he smiled, reassuring her, making her almost giddy.

"Yes, I agree to no premarital sex and wedding bells are not out of the question."

She grinned at him, her heart racing. Maybe Cupid was working for them. "So, when is our next date?"

"This Friday at Jim and Shadow's rehearsal dinner. I'd love if you were my date."

"What should I wear?"

CHAPTER 6

*C*hloe sat next to Kelsey, Drew's younger sister, at the rehearsal dinner. The woman's interest was obvious when she found out her brother had brought her as his date.

"Jim rescued Shadow after he did the Cupid dance," Kelsey whispered. "And the same for me and Cody. He picked me up after running the statue. In fact, I think all our friends and family met after dancing naked around the fountain."

An uncomfortable feeling overcame Chloe. She wanted to confide in his sister, but being the preacher's daughter, no way would she tell her how she and Drew bumped into each other. If that story reached her father's ears or her surrogate mothers, they would hold a prayer vigil in her front yard.

As it was, she often wondered if they weren't already praying, hoping she would find someone to love. Especially her father with the men he sent her way. Fortunately, the trickle of nerds had slowed. Finally, he had gotten her message. Let her find her own man.

"You were the first woman Drew saw after he did the Cupid dance?" Kelsey blurted out.

No harm in telling her that much.

"Yes, I was Drew's first after doing the dance."

"Oh, tell me what happened?" his sister said.

Chloe shifted uneasily in the chair. Kelsey was nice, but she couldn't tell her the truth. All she could admit to was running into Drew after his dance and she hoped everyone assumed they met after he put his clothes back on.

"Oh, look, I think the boys are going to do the first toast," Chloe said, trying to draw her attention away from her and Drew.

Cody stood. "Shadow and Jim, as we prepare to celebrate your special day, you need to thank me for this happy event. Our little wager has now found forever after for three of the four of you."

The small group laughed. "The four of us have been friends for a long time. None of us believed in this God of Love superstition, but because Kelsey and her girlfriends danced, I'm now happily engaged and you're getting married. May your lives be rich with happiness, blessed with children, and happily ever after. To Jim and Shadow."

Everyone raised their wine glasses. Chloe was happy for the couple, yet part of her twinged with jealousy of the love she could see shining from their eyes when they glanced at one another. Chloe wanted that same kind of love for her and Drew.

Ryan Jones stood. "I'd like to say as sheriff, I don't condone this dancing without your clothes around the statue, but I, too, am a happily married man because of that silly rock in the town square. To Jim and Shadow, may your days be joyous and your nights filled with love."

They all laughed and lifted their glasses.

Kyle rose from his seat. "To Jim and Shadow. Jim, love has been a long time coming. Frankly, after watching Shadow and you together, you couldn't have found a more perfect woman. Shadow helps you relax and live a little and you give Shadow stability. On this journey of life, may your days be many, your life be overflowing with love and happiness and rugrats. Congrats!"

SYLVIA MCDANIEL

The crowd cheered as they clinked champagne flutes. Then it was Drew's turn.

"How many of you here have been affected by this superstition?"

Drew was asking this question? That surprised her after his earlier comments about his own Cupid experience.

Swallowing hard, Chloe stared in shock at the number of people who hoisted their hands. Could it be that Cupid would show her and Drew they were meant to be together?

With a longing gaze at Drew tonight, she had watched him interact with his brothers, taking pictures with Jim and Shadow. So many things about him drew her to him. She liked his intelligence, his wit, his persistence - she didn't like his one-night stands. But even that had changed. After all, he confessed he had not slept with a woman in six months.

"I'm shocked," he said. "In order to fulfill a bet, I did the Cupid dance and the first woman I ran into was the lovely Chloe who is here with me. Tonight is not about me and Chloe, but Jim and Shadow."

Pausing for a moment, he turned to his new sister-in-law. "Shadow, when Jim introduced you, I thought he struck gold. You're the right person for my brother and I'm happy he's found someone to spend his life with. Jim, you've become the patriarch of our family and taken on responsibilities to keep our business going. We're proud of you and honored to call you brother. May the two of you live long and prosper and fill that big old empty house with lots of babies for me to spoil."

Chloe's eyes pricked with tears. Could the Cupid statue and returning to the town change Drew? Maybe the bad boy was beginning to realize long lasting relationships mattered most in life. Not just fleeting fly byes in the night. Maybe, just maybe, soon, he would look at her with love in his eyes.

THE NEXT DAY at the wedding reception, Drew watched his sister and sister-in-law tag team Chloe with the bouquet. Shadow aimed right for her and Kelsey played linebacker making certain no one had a chance but Chloe who looked mortified.

Not only was everyone trying to put the two of them as the next engaged couple, but they acted like she should be thrilled she tamed the bad boy.

They both knew that wasn't true, and in fact, Drew had already turned one girl down this afternoon. This new dating arrangement was still so new and fragile for them, they were fumbling their way through a major life event together. The women he went out with were well versed in what to expect.

Chloe was different. It was one of the things that drew him to her. Before they left her house, she warned him just so they were clear, she wouldn't accept his hound dogging ways. If she even caught a glimpse of him flirting and carrying on with another woman, he would receive a swift kick in the rear and a resounding goodbye. The woman didn't play around.

Her morals were simple. One man, one woman with a ring on her finger vowed to each other for a lifetime. A partnership she planned on lasting forever.

While it seemed like a simple enough pledge, Drew was not sure he could uphold to her high standards. Shocking, he agreed with her and that's why he never pursued a real, honest relationship - his way everything was superficial.

The only promises made lasted the night and not the rest of time.

For his own good, he needed to change, but part of him resisted giving up his freedom. When a man took a wife, he made a vow to honor, protect, support her, and their children in sickness and health.

In his line of work, examples of men who failed at that job miserably were too numerous to count. A lot of women failed as well. Nasty divorces, lunatic break-ups, and meanness the likes of which he'd never considered.

If he promised a woman forever, he would die honoring those vows. The carefree playboy had no commitments except to himself. The husband had responsibilities to those he loved. Falling in love was harder than a quick tumble between the sheets.

Walking over to where Chloe stood, taking pictures with the bouquet, he grinned at her. Standing beside Shadow, Chloe appeared stunning and he could imagine her in a lacy white dress. His chest squeezed and he reminded himself they were dating. Nothing more.

"Poor girl," an older woman watching nearby said to her friend. "Absolutely, she has the worst luck with men. Always chooses the wrong one. And now that lawyer and her? He's a player chasing after the good girl."

Yes, he pursued Chloe. No longer did he want to be known as the bad boy in town. Before his gigolo ways had been a status symbol, but now, he no longer wanted to be that guy. The local Othello.

"I know," the other woman said. "Chloe was devastated when she caught Austin cheating on her. She'll soon find this one between some woman's legs."

Drew fought the urge to defend himself against the old biddy, but realized he would come out looking like the loser. Taking a deep breath, he released it slowly, nothing should ruin his brother's big day.

Finally, the photographer had enough and walked away. Drew stepped around the little old ladies wanting them to know he heard every word.

"Hey, look at you," he said, approaching the woman he couldn't stop thinking about. Right now, she seemed a little frazzled and that surprised him. Always in the past, she'd been so certain of herself.

She handed him the souvenir flowers and picked up her glass of champagne, taking a big gulp. "Next time I attend any of your family weddings, would you please remind me of how your sister and sisters-in-law can be so determined. Honestly, Drew, I was trying to downplay our relationship, not draw attention to us."

A grin spread across his face. Both of them were dealing with the anxiety of being seen in public as a couple. "Well, my toast last night didn't help, but maybe it's for the best. Now at least everyone knows we're seeing each other."

They could stop guessing who the first woman was he met after dancing around the fountain. And those blue-haired grannies would see that he was the right man for Chloe, at this moment.

"Why should that matter?" she asked.

"Because being with you makes me a better man. What I don't understand is why you like to be with me?" he said, wondering what besides her belief in the superstition kept her seeing him.

The sweet upturn of her lips into a teasing smile sent tremors through him. "Well, certainly not your looks. Every woman in town is after them. I want something more."

"Like what?" he asked, smiling at her response.

"Your brilliant mind," she said and leaned over and kissed him. For some reason her words made him want to scoop her into his arms and carry her to the nearest bed, but that wouldn't happen.

"Hey, you two, save it for the wedding night," Jim said to them in front of everyone, making Drew groan. Why did his brother have to ruin a perfectly great kiss?

"I'm about to toss the garter."

Releasing his lips, Chloe smiled at him, sending ripples of awareness straight to his groin, her blue eyes warm. "Your turn to be humiliated."

TWO DAYS LATER, Drew sat with Cody at Valentino's bar, sipping a cold one. Today, Drew was stunned to receive a message from Chloe - 'Got a call from Austin, be back in a couple days.'

Was this how it felt when he dumped a woman? Why would she openly admit she went to see Austin after they'd decided to date?

Cody stared at him. "Man, I was surprised as hell to hear you come out and tell everyone you and Chloe were dating. Last I heard, you weren't ever going to get serious."

Even his friends didn't want him to reform. They all thought he lived a wonderful life. What they didn't think about was the loneliness, the fear of disease, and the awkwardness of getting naked with a stranger. Really, being promiscuous wasn't a glamorous life like they envisioned.

"I'm trying to change. We agreed to see each other, and today, I receive a cryptic voicemail saying she was going to visit Austin."

"No way. Not Austin, the associate pastor at her father's church? She caught him cheating during a marital counseling session with a married woman," Cody said, shocked. "That congregation just about ran him out of town. No way, man."

Drew turned. If his friend new about Austin, then the whole town knew the man cheated. "Why would Chloe go back to him?"

This was the first time she gave any inclination that she might have that crazy woman gene. The one so many of his clients seemed to have, where they took back the rotten husband after he'd stolen their savings to go off with another woman.

Cody turned to him and shook his head. "Are you certain you understood right? Something is off. Are you guys exclusive? He's the last man on earth I'd think she'd go back to. This doesn't seem right. But you know Karma is a bitch. How many times did you do this to other women?"

"We're not talking about my past. We're talking about how I'm changing."

How long would it take before people realized he turned a new leaf?

"Doesn't feel good when it happens to you, does it?" Cody said.

Drew glanced at his friend. "You've been zero, squat, kind of help here tonight. I hoped you would help me understand why she would go back to a man like Austin, when I'm here."

Picking up his beer, Cody grinned at Drew. "You do realize you're falling hard. Cupid aimed for your heart and his arrow has struck. You're acting like a man bitten by love. You're acting like a jealous lover."

Drew cringed inside. If this was love, he didn't like the feeling. The thought of Chloe possibly sleeping with Austin made him sick to his stomach. For a moment, he considered jumping in his car and going after her.

"Maybe I should go after her."

"Maybe you should sit back and learn why she's gone to Austin. It could be innocent."

"This doesn't seem innocent. Feels like my girl is two-timing me."

Cody laughed so hard, he had tears in his eyes. Finally, he stopped took a swig of his beer. "Like I said, Karma, she's a bitch and Cupid is about to slam you hard."

CHAPTER 7

*C*hloe had been shocked to receive the call asking her to interview for a remodeling job in Austin, Texas. It wasn't often you were given the opportunity to talk to the historical association about how you would remodel an older home.

There were many presenters and she didn't know if she impressed the organization enough to earn the position, but showing her designs had been an honor. She couldn't wait to tell Drew about the old house and the stuffed shirts in the historical society.

Now back in Cupid, she was amazed at how much work her crew finished on the Perkins homestead. The rewiring was complete, the plumbing almost done, and some of the walls were taped and floated. The painter left a sample book and the tile guy was ready to pick flooring. The old house was starting to come together.

On the way home from Austin, she called Drew and he sounded odd. Arriving at any moment, she felt excited to share her news and see him.

When he walked in the door, she hurried over to greet him,

giving him a quick kiss and a hug. Stiffening in her arms, she pulled back and glanced at him. "Oh my goodness, I missed you."

Stepping out of her embrace he glared at her. What happened while she was away? In the matter of just forty-eight hours, he'd gone from suitor to withdrawing from her.

"Miss me? I think there is someone else you want more."

"What are you talking about," she said, confusion rippling through her.

"Why did you visit Austin?"

Relief flooded through her like a waterfall. For a moment, she feared he would break up with her. The thought that one of his lady loves convinced him to return and she lost him forever.

"Why did you leave me to go to Austin."

"The historical society wanted to see my vision for this house" she said confused.

His face relaxed and he sighed. Then it dawned on her. Did he think she went back to Austin, the pastoral assistant? Like a slow burn, outrage rippled through her and the tension gripped her hands, causing them to clench.

"You think I would go back to that two-timing, low-life worthless piece of garbage who I caught having sex?" she said, her voice rising. "Are you crazy?"

"You said Austin," he said, his voice tense as he ran his hand through his hair. "All I could think was that you went back to *him*, not the city."

How could anyone think she would take back that man. The hurt, the humiliation, the sight of seeing him plunging into that woman she could never forget. No, she would die a shriveled up old maid before Austin came back into her life. What if he feared she would do to him, what he had done to some of his girlfriends?

"That's about as lame as an excuse as I've ever heard. Could it be you assumed I was doing what you've done to other women."

"No," he denied, but the guilty look on his face confirmed her suspicions.

"Your face tells me otherwise."

Sighing he shook his head. "Cody said the same thing last night."

"How in the world are you a successful lawyer if you can't school your expressions when you lie?"

"I'm a fine attorney capable of schooling my expressions, except around you," he said softly.

That admission blew all the frustration and anger building inside Chloe right out the window. A warmth filled her, leaving her glowing with happiness.

A grin spread across her face and she laughed. "Good, I'll always recognize when you're lying."

"Yes, I know," he said, smiling at her.

Walking up to him, she poked her finger in his chest. "I'll make you this promise. Never will you have to worry about me cheating on you. Until the day we either part ways amicably or death separates us, I will not cheat on you. Erase that concern. On the other hand, you are the one I have misgivings about."

He took her in his arms. "I'll make you the same promise. Never worry about me cheating on you. Until the day we either part amicably or death parts us, I will be faithful to you."

It seemed, they just made their first vows to one another and it left her feeling giddy inside. Already she could feel herself falling for Drew and that both frightened and exhilarated her.

Maybe something good had come out of this misunderstanding.

"Now, it's time for you to get laid," she said, whispering in his ear.

Jerking back, eyes wide, he stared at her and she smiled. "Your tile that is."

❧

EVERY YEAR CHLOE volunteered at the local father-daughter dance. One of the most enjoyable ways she gave back to the community and free advertising, since she was one of the sponsors. The organizer of the event placed her at the punch bowl alongside Kelsey.

She would've asked Drew to spend the evening here with her so she had someone to talk to, but he had plans for the evening.

"I'm shocked to see you here," Kelsey said.

"You're here for the same reason I am. The publicity," she said, remembering the ad for Kelsey's shop in the program.

Chloe liked Drew's sister. After learning about their Cupid experience, the woman accepted and treated her almost like family.

"Yes, hopefully the fathers might find something nice for the mother of their child."

Normally this wasn't a fun evening. Now Chloe had someone to share the time with and she was looking forward to the evening even without Drew.

"Or they might consider my company for their next remodel job," Chloe said. "But really, I enjoy watching the little girls and their dads."

Standing behind the table, they handed out cups of sweet juice and cookies to the kids when they tired.

Kelsey turned and gave her a strange glance. "Why didn't you tell me Drew's here. And he's dancing with that cute little black girl."

"Because I didn't know he was here," Chloe responded bewildered. Why was Drew at the father-daughter dance? A trickle of alarm spiral down to her stomach. They'd made a vow to one another and already he'd broken it? "Who is the child's mother?"

"No clue," Kelsey said.

Watching the two made Chloe's heart race with fear. Being the dutiful date, Drew was attentive to the little girl, who looked up at him and smiled, her eyes lighting up with delight. Together the two twirled around the floor and her heart ached. Drew would be a wonderful father.

"He doesn't have children, does he?" She couldn't help but ask his sister.

"Not that I've been told," Kelsey said and turned to the volunteer on the other side of her. "What is the name of the child with my brother?"

The woman said something to her and Chloe fought the urge to keep from shoving her way into the conversation. Finally, Kelsey turned back to her.

"Did he ever mention Marissa?"

"Never," Chloe said, racking her brain.

"She's the daughter of Arial McFadden."

"Do you know Arial? Has she ever dated Drew?" Chloe asked, knowing she sounded jealous, but she didn't care.

"No, they were classmates in high school. I'd bet my boutique and all I love, this little girl is not Drew's."

Observing Drew with the beautiful child who obviously knew him made Chloe nervous. Never had he mentioned a child or a child's mother or even what he was doing tonight. She assumed he was working on a case. Much to her surprise, he was here where fathers brought their daughters to their first dance.

Just then, he strolled up to the table, his eyes widening at the sight of Kelsey and Chloe.

"Ladies, I didn't expect to find you here."

"We didn't plan on seeing you here, either," Chloe said, trying to keep the tension from her voice, but failing miserably.

"I'd like you to meet my date. Marissa McFadden."

"Hello, Marissa, you look very pretty," Chloe said.

"Thanks, my mom helped me pick out this dress."

Only five or six years old, Chloe wasn't about to put a child in the middle of something she didn't understand. Surely, he had an explanation.

"Let's go dance again, Dad," Marissa said.

"Sure," Drew said and glanced back over his shoulder mouthing the words to Chloe and his sister. "I can explain."

Kelsey whispered, "Now I remember who she is."

Chloe smiled at him the grin she reserved for the cheaters, losers, men she wanted out of her life. When he walked far enough away, she said. "You better be able to justify how this little girl calls you dad."

❧

DREW WAS IN TROUBLE. How could he turn down helping an innocent child, and if Chloe was still upset after his explanation, then they weren't meant to be together. In hindsight, he realized if he'd told her, she would have been prepared to see him with Marissa.

This relationship thing was trickier than he expected. Book smart and people smart, but in relationships, he was dumber than a box of rocks.

Driving up in front of the bed and breakfast, Chloe's car was parked in the drive, and she sat waiting on the hood for him. Reckoning time.

"It's a sad day when I'm jealous of a six-year-old," she said as he crawled out of his car.

Laughing at the idea of her being envious, he held up his hand. "Wait, I have a perfectly good reason."

"Start talking, buddy, or I'll get out my Chinese torture tools."

"Oh no, not the tools," he said, walking up to her and kissing her on the lips. Lingering, he didn't want to stop there, but she waited to hear him explain why he took Marissa to the father-daughter dance.

"A friend of mine in school, Ariel McFadden, and her partner Scarlet McFadden wanted to adopt a foster child. They asked me to be their attorney and I handled their adoption.

"During the process, I became friends with the little girl.

83

Scarlet travels a lot for her job, and they worried about the kids making fun of Marissa if one of them went with her. When Marissa asked me if I would go to the dance with her. I couldn't deny that sweetheart.

"Abandoned by her opium addicted mother, with no record of who is her father, she's seen the worst and the best of humanity. With Ariel and Scarlet, she has a great home. This kid has come so far and didn't want to be bullied by kids. I--"

Chloe's mouth covered his and she kissed him hard, her hands gripping his head and bringing his lips solidly against her own. He didn't resist. In fact, he laid her on the car top, covering her body with his, his mouth ravishing hers, taking control.

Tonight, seeing her give out punch, he knew there would be questions, doubts, and yet she kissed him before they finished talking. With his last breath, he hoped this implied she understood, she accepted how he helped this little girl. His reputation was bad enough, decent women doubted him and he couldn't help but wonder if she did, too.

Finally, they came up for air, her breathing harsh as she gazed at him in the moonlight.

"My only request is I wish you had told me," she said. "If I had known, I would have approved and never been envious of a first grader."

It wasn't the kind of defense he would be proud of, as she was right. Still, he never told anyone his whereabouts and taking a child to a dance didn't seem such a big deal. Lying on top of her, he longed to concentrate only on Chloe.

"As soon as I spotted you," Drew said, "I thought, *you crazy fool, why didn't you tell her?* In my exoneration, I'm not used to telling women what I'm doing or where I'm going. In the future, I will tell you my plans. I give you my word."

Pulling his head down close to hers. "Please, tell me. That's all I ask, but frankly, what you did for that child was awesome. Every little girl wants to belong with the other kids and sometimes circumstances make that impossible. What you did gave her the biggest smile. You're this little girl's hero."

Her mouth covered his once again and she leaned into his kiss, her breasts smashed against his chest, sending heat spiraling through him as his penis hardened between the V of her legs.

The taste of passion and desire and a tiny bit of sweetness oozed from her lips. Nothing could make him happier than to take her upstairs and bed her, but where he was staying was gossip central in Cupid. In fact, he wouldn't be a bit surprised Mabel had her nose crushed against the window watching.

Though her father wouldn't be pleased, Drew was enjoying this moment.

His hand came between them and he cupped her breast and she moaned deeply in her throat. The touch of her nipple beneath his hand left him heady with craving. Every day, he wanted her more. Every night he wanted it all, but her father...

Releasing her flesh, he gave her a butterfly kiss, slowly letting his lips trail towards her ear. "Mabel is getting quite a show from us. Even now the phone lines are burning up with her blathering about how she watched us making out on your car."

"The woman is probably asleep. Regardless, I need to get home."

"Well, if Mabel isn't watching, maybe we should continue," he said, nipping at her neck, feeling her shudder at the feel of his mouth.

"Maybe that would find us both in trouble," she said sighing.

"I like trouble," he said, pressing into her.

"I know you do," she replied. "Your kind of danger requires a ring."

In her eyes, yes. Still, when he pulled in here and observed her waiting for him, he thought there would be a fight on his hands. Instead, they made out. The woman kept him guessing. "Always a stickler for details."

"Absolutely," she said and softly kissed him on the lips as she pushed him off her. "Sleep well, Drew."

"Damn woman, you know how to leave a man hurting."

"Better aching, than trapped."

With a sigh, he said, "So logical. One day, I'm going to make you realize how much you're missing."

"When I'm not just a challenge and a lasting emotion exists between us, with a band on my left hand, then I'll be ready and willing to be in your bed. Then you can show me *everything*." She smiled in the darkness. "Goodnight, Drew."

Swallowing to curb the heat engulfing him, he sighed. She wanted him to show her what she was missing. That he could do all night long.

CHAPTER 8

*T*he next morning, her cell rang and Chloe answered it before she finished taking her measurements.

"Chloe, how are you?" Mrs. Gibson, one of her surrogate mothers asked. "I've been worried about your father. His color looks a little peaked. Is he feeling all right."

"As far as I know, he's fine," Chloe responded, wondering how to end this conversation as soon as possible. Right in the middle of designing a backsplash when her phone buzzed, she wished she hadn't answered.

"Watch over him. I'm concerned," she said.

"Always," she said. "He's all I have left."

"Yes, I understand." There was a lengthy pause and Chloe was about to tell her she had to hang up, when the real reason for the call came out.

"Dear, I hear you've been seeing Drew Lawrence. Your mother would not approve of you being associated with him. That man dates fast women and expects them to sleep with him on the first date."

A fire began to grow in Chloe. A small ember caught flame and rapidly consumed her. Why did the women in the congregation think who she dated was any of their business? She would see who she damn well pleased. And using her mother's memory, oh no.

"How do you know?"

"Well, that's what that type of man does. Those men switch women like they change underwear. A nice girl like you deserves someone better."

The rage burning inside her grew hotter by the minute. How could anyone evolve when people wouldn't let you become a better person?

"Tell me, who has he gone out with since he returned to Cupid?" Chloe asked, trying to keep her emotions out of her voice.

There was silence.

"No one besides you."

"Exactly. Did you ever consider he wants to be different? Drew is attending church."

"Just to get to you."

Chloe wanted to slam her phone down at the narrow mindedness of people. Drew would never change if the people wouldn't accept he no longer was the town gigolo.

"Now, Mrs. Gibson, how can you say that? We're not supposed to judge. Come to me with concrete facts, then we'll discuss Drew's antics."

"True, but that boy's a player and he's making a move on you. It seems like you're falling for him."

For a moment, she thought she was going to spew right there in the phone. The woman would not give up and mind her own business. Somehow, she had to accept the fact not everyone would be happy with her dating Drew, and frankly, she didn't give a fig.

"If it's the right move and he doesn't try to seduce me, then I think those are pretty good moves."

Silence echoed over the airwaves. "Did I tell you my nephew George is coming into town next week."

No way would Chloe go out with her relatives. The man might be the best-looking gentleman in the city and she would be busy cleaning her toilets that night because of his aunt.

"Wonderful. Shame I already have plans with Drew."

At that moment, Drew walked in the door carrying lunch. As he came through the door, smiling, he waved with his arms loaded down with sacks. Right now, he looked like a knight in shining armor with his hands filled with food.

"Thanks for the call, Mrs. Gibson. Drew just came in, bringing me lunch. What a kind man. See you this Sunday."

Chloe hung up, seething mad. People could be so unforgiving.

"Problems?"

"One of the nosy surrogate mothers wanting me to go out with her nephew and warning me about you."

Laughing, he said, "And it sounds like you set her straight."

"You bet I did. Nosy old biddy."

After setting the food down, Drew came to her and wrapped his arms around her and kissed her on the lips, sending a shiver down her spine. The image of them sprawled on top of her car and how far they'd gone the night before had her pressing against him.

For the first time in her life, she'd actually desired to be with a man. Every day, she fell a little more for Drew. Every day he did unexpected things that made her realize he was a great man. A man deserving of love.

They broke apart, both breathing heavily as she stared into emerald eyes that reminded her of forests and evergreen trees. The man was handsome as sin on a stick and she was finding it harder and harder to deny she wanted him.

"Lunchtime," he said. "If you have time, we might go over some of the samples of tile and help me choose."

"Thank you. Why are you always so thoughtful?"

He gave her a quick kiss on the tip of the nose. "Because I like doing things for you. It makes me feel good. There is something so sexy hearing you defend me, which makes me hot."

A rush of warmth went through Chloe and she wondered again why she refused to have sex with this man. "Thanks, Drew, one of the biggest ways to show a woman you love or care for her is to put her needs first. You do that very well."

Grinning at her, he said, "I try. Now, let's eat this meal I picked up and then get started picking out the tile. I'm ready to move in here."

Chloe pushed Mrs. Gibson's call from her mind and quickly laid out their spread. More and more, she wanted this man. At this moment, she was almost ready to throw caution to the wind and sleep with Drew.

But again, her practical side reminded her, not yet.

❧

TWO DAYS LATER, Drew stepped into the local bank to tend to business regarding his construction loan. As he strolled into the old building, he noticed a group of people surrounding a man down on the floor.

Walking up to the teller, he tried to figure out what was happening.

"What's going on?" he asked.

"Reverend Kilian fainted dead away. They're trying to revive him," she said, a worried expression on her face.

Drew cursed, his heart leaping into his chest. "Excuse me, he's my girlfriend's father."

Rushing to where Chloe's father lay sprawled on his back, Drew noted his breathing was labored, his color white. Fear gripped Drew's stomach as he gazed at the man. Uncaring, he moved people aside to kneel beside him.

"Reverend, wake up," he called close to his ear.

"He's out," a woman said, wringing her hands. "An ambulance is on the way."

"Good," Drew said and lifted the man's hand checking his pulse. A steady beat pumped beneath his thumb, which relieved him.

Shaking the older man's shoulder, he attempted to arouse him. "Reverend, it's Drew."

The man groaned and blinked his eyes a couple of times. "Drew?"

"You're in the bank. You passed out. Do you hurt?"

The man moaned and his eyes fluttered shut. This didn't look good. Yes, the man was sick, but hopefully he had months. Time that Drew needed him here, helping him, guiding him with regards to Chloe.

The ambulance pulled up outside, lights and sirens sounding. In less than a minute, a very capable paramedic moved everyone back. Drew made room for him.

"How long has he been out?" the paramedic asked, leaning down beside him, putting his stethoscope to his chest.

"About five minutes the second time. For a moment, he opened his eyes and responded, calling me by name before he went out again," Drew said, thinking he must find Chloe.

The paramedic took his vitals and turned to Drew. "We're taking him to the hospital. From this initial exam, his lungs sound congested and he needs medical attention. Do you know his next of kin?"

"Yes, I'll pick up his daughter and meet you at the emergency room," Drew said, rising.

The time for her father to tell her the truth arrived in the form of a trip in an ambulance. Even if the old man still had time, she needed to learn about her father's illness and prepare for his eventual death. A process he didn't envy her one bit. A process where he would be beside her the entire way.

SYLVIA MCDANIEL

"Thanks," the paramedic said, standing, making room for the stretcher.

Drew hurried out the door, his business all but forgotten. Jumping in his car, he tried to remain calm while he drove the two blocks to Chloe's house.

Yes, the old man was dying of pancreatic cancer, but he hadn't told Chloe. The man wanted her engaged or married before he died. That was his wish and he patiently waited on Drew.

Drew recognized he wasn't ready to ask Chloe to marry him. Only two weeks ago, they agreed to see each other and now he felt pressure to take their relationship to the next level. He had no clue what that entailed.

To ask for her hand in marriage and promise her a ring and forever sent panic radiating through his body. Enough for him to consider bolting back to Dallas. Yet, he didn't want to leave Chloe to face this alone. And there was his agreement to date the pastor's daughter.

Pulling up in front of his grandmother's house, he saw her truck sitting in the driveway. Leaving the car on, he jumped out and sprinted up the steps to the inside.

"Chloe," he yelled.

Coming around the entrance to the kitchen, she stared at him. "Drew, what's wrong."

"Drop your tools and come with me. They've taken your dad to the hospital."

"Oh no," she ran back and grabbed her purse. Seconds later, they were out the door and she closed and locked it behind them.

"What happened," she said, almost running to the car.

"Your father collapsed at the bank this morning. When I came in, he was prostrate on the ground. The ambulance had been called by the time I arrived."

"Is he all right?"

How could he answer this question? Her father should tell her what was going on, not Drew. At this moment, he needed to support her and hope this was a portent for her father to be honest with his daughter.

"I don't know. The paramedics took him to the hospital. The man told me it sounded like his lungs were congested, but they weren't taking any chances. When they wheeled him out the door, he was on oxygen. That's when I came to get you."

Biting her lip, she was quiet the short distance to the small town's hospital.

"He can't leave me," she finally said. "Not now."

Drew reached over and took her hand and squeezed it tightly. What could you say that would bring someone comfort when they had no idea what they were about to face?

An ache centered in his chest at the pain he knew she would soon be facing and he wanted to protect, console, and help her deal with the grieving. No matter what, he wanted to be there for Chloe.

⚜

FOR OVER THREE HOURS, her father lay in the emergency room before they decided to admit him. Now, she waited for him to be transferred to his room. Hopefully, soon she would have an opportunity to talk to the doctor and ask questions.

When they wheeled him past her down the hall toward his room, she couldn't help but think how old he appeared. White hair stuck to his head and his skin a pasty pale, he'd never looked so bad. Fear gripped her stomach and rose in her throat.

At fifty-nine, she didn't consider him that old. Already her mother had left her, if he died, she would be alone.

Taking a deep breath, she released her anxiety. A simple case of chest congestion, nothing to worry about. Something that a dose of antibiotics wouldn't cure. Chiding herself, she tried to calm her irrational panic. Her father would be around to bounce his grandbabies on his knee. God would never be so cruel as to take him from her.

Following his stretcher, Drew held her hand as they walked behind. Once they were in the room, they moved him onto the bed, then the nurses came in and checked his vital signs.

Soon, the room emptied, but for her and Drew. Walking to his side, the rhythmic sound of the machines comforting and disturbing at the same time, she grabbed her father's hand.

"Dad, why didn't you tell me you were feeling bad?"

"It just happened," he said, gazing at her, his face a sickly shade of white. "Standing in line at the bank and the next thing I know, Drew is kneeling beside me. The doctor told me I have pneumonia."

Chloe sighed, remembering Mrs. Gibson's call warning her that her father looked bad. Could something else be wrong or did he need to slow down. There was no way she could think that something serious might be amiss with him.

"You've been working too hard. You need more rest."

"If I slow down, I might die," he said with a smile.

"If you don't, you'll die and leave me," she said squeezing his hand. "I want you here, Daddy."

She hadn't called her father *daddy* since she was a young kid and the words brought tears to his eyes.

His voice choked up. "Chloe, we all go to be with the Father. My time will come and I don't know the hour."

"Not yet," she said. "You're middle age and I need you here."

As much as they argued over her choice of career, the men she dated, and the fact she wasn't in church every time the doors opened, didn't mean she didn't love him. While she tried to make a life of her own, she still adhered to the basic principles of her upbringing.

Being a preacher's daughter was not easy. Each time she screwed up in life, the whole congregation learned and someone ran to tell her father.

The tattle telling grew old. Their interference was the main reason she had taken a step back from the parish, only showing up on Sunday.

"Sometimes we don't get what we want. Honey, if it's my time to go, then at least I'll be joining your mother. This is why I've been praying you would find a man. Before I die, I want to walk you down the aisle and hand you over to your husband. Maybe even hold my grandchildren. I'm not going anywhere until the good Lord says come home."

Smiling at him, she leaned over and kissed him on the cheek. "Rest, Daddy. Rest and get better."

"Yes, you go home. All day you had to sit out in that waiting room." He turned to Drew. "Thank you for your help today. Take care of my daughter."

A strange look passed from her father to Drew and she turned and glanced at them both. Why did there seem to be this weird communication, especially when her father didn't even like Drew and would prefer that she didn't see him.

"No problem, sir. I'll make certain Chloe gets home," he said.

"One less thing for me to worry about," her father said.

How would her father react if he knew that she had bumped into Drew dancing naked around the Cupid statue? According to the legend he was her true love. What a tangled web and yet she didn't want her father concerned about anything but getting well.

For her, Drew had once again gone above and beyond, helping her father and racing to find her and staying at her side while she stood by for three hours for her father to be moved from the ER to a room. Drew sat right beside her, calming her when she started to become overwhelmed.

The man was winning her heart and proving to her he was not only a good man, but her man. Chloe wanted to sleep with Drew. The desire between them felt explosive, but she still felt uncertain. The man was a player. Maybe a reformed player that she was rapidly falling for. Should she take a chance on Drew?

$\mathcal{U}$neasiness slithered up Drew's spine. Two weeks had passed since Chloe's father's bout of pneumonia and the man now rested at home. Chloe had invited Drew over to her house for supper, telling him she wanted to fix spaghetti and hating to fix a huge pot for herself.

Together, they had laughed and talked while eating the delicious pasta and even had a couple of glasses of wine. The whole atmosphere seemed like a seduction and that's what made him a little nervous.

Not that he didn't want to bed Chloe. Oh no, he had dreams of the two of them together, wrapped in each other's arms, her moaning and him plunging deeply within her. Only, he woke up, his breathing harsh, his dick hard and pulsating in his lonely bed.

Yes, he wanted Chloe, but he also wanted to be a different man. Not the man whore he was known for, but rather a good man who felt uncertain about marriage and forever after. There was no way to get one without the other and was where his confusion stemmed from.

"Dishes are in the dishwasher," she said, sinking down beside him. "Thanks for coming over and letting me cook. Occasionally,

I have these spurts of domestication. Not often, so I need to take advantage of them when they occur."

Wanting her closer, he put his arm around the back of her couch and pulled her into his side. "You're a domestic goddess. Let me know the next time you want to cook. I'll buy the groceries."

Laughing, she smiled at him. "Hardly. There is nothing better than a home cooked meal."

She picked up a remote and music played in the background.

Was he being tested or was she honestly trying to seduce him? Either way, he knew he was too weak to sustain an advanced assault. Still, if he remained true to the Drew he was becoming, he would never let her entice him now.

Her hand reached over and pulled his head down to meet her lips. The press of her soft mouth over his own, intoxicating and sweet as his body reacted to the rush of pleasure. Pushing her down on the sofa, he lay on top of her.

The crush of her breasts hard against his chest with only their clothes separating them was almost his undoing. While his analytical brain began to give him the odds on his chances of taking her virginity, his mouth continued to evoke moans from her.

Just one touch was all he needed and he would break away. Just a chance to run his fingertips along the satin creaminess of her breast, the hard ridges of her nipple. All he wanted was something to add to his tortured dreams and then he would stop. But not yet.

Reaching beneath her blouse, his fingers shoved her bra out of the way, searching for the full roundness of her breast. The silkiness of her skin, the ripe fullness of her bust and he moaned knowing he should cease, but not ready to. Just a little more.

Pressing his hardened dick into her mound, she groaned and broke their kiss.

"Drew," she gasped.

Now she would tell him to stop. With every caress, he waited for her signal and now she would tell him enough.

"Chloe," he said, his mouth trailing kisses down her neck, his hands caressing her flesh.

"Don't stop," she cried. "Please keep going. I want to."

Desire raged through his blood like snow melt in spring rushing through him, churning and boiling and there was no way he would slow down. Oh, how he longed to continue. Fingers trailed down the front of her blouse as he pushed the garment up, his mouth closed over her hardened kernel as he gently suckled her breast.

"Drew, please, don't stop," she moaned.

What the hell? All the while, he was trying his best not to lose control, she wanted him to go on. She wanted to have sex with him. Tonight she planned this seduction for him to take her virginity right here and now. And he would gladly take her up on that offer.

Gripping her head with one hand, his fingers reached for her pants until he reached the waistband of her panties. As his digits dived inside, seeking her center, his conscious awakened from its nap.

Wasn't he leading her down the same path as the rest of his girlfriends? Seduce them, have sex with them and then discard them? Wasn't that the actions of the old Drew? Didn't he want to be different? And if pigs could fly, wouldn't he be a rich man? Crap, he had to stop.

Slowly, he pulled his hands out of her pants and yanked down her shirt, but not before one last lingering glance of her naked breasts.

"We can't," he groaned "We can wait."

For a moment, she stilled, their breaths harsh in the darkness. "Don't you desire me?"

He pressed into her. "Can't you feel how hard you make me? Lately, I dream of you at night. I want you so badly, but I don't want you to be like all the other girls I dated. If this is going to work, it has to be different. Different means, we wait."

Tears were in the corners of her eyes as she stared up at him in shock. "Oh."

Suddenly her front door opened and her father strolled into the house. "Chloe, are you here? Saw your car outside and decided to drop in. Why aren't the lights on?"

Oh, crap it's her father.

☙

CHLOE SCRAMBLED to get her clothes rearranged hoping they didn't appear too disheveled.

"Dad, what are you doing here?" she asked as she switched on the light. Yes, she was an adult, but still to be almost caught by her father at any age was embarrassing.

"Drew, I didn't know you were here," he said frowning. "Maybe it's a good thing I came when I did. Remember what I told you with regards to my daughter."

Huh? Drew and her father had talked? What did that mean?

"Yes, sir, we were sitting here talking. Part of the dating ritual, learning about your partner."

Embarrassed beyond belief, she just wanted this little scene to end. "Did you need something, Dad? Are you feeling okay?"

"Better every day. I wanted to come by and talk for a few moments, but it can wait. You've got company."

Drew stood and offered her father, his seat. "Oh no, sir, I was getting ready to leave. Tomorrow is a big meeting on a divorce I'm working on. The night before I always like to go over my notes about what's best for my client."

What was going on between her father and Drew. It almost seemed like they were friends. And they never had been before.

"Understand. See you in church on Sunday," he said, sinking down onto Chloe's couch.

Standing, she said, "I'll walk you out."

"Come by the rectory and let's drink coffee sometime," her father called and her head almost swiveled. What? Dad had invited Drew for coffee? The apocalypse should happen any day now.

"Will do," Drew responded and a tingle of disbelief scurried through her. Since the hospital, the two men appeared to like each other. Odd.

At the door, she followed Drew outside on the porch.

Pulling her into his arms, he smiled down at her. "The spaghetti tasted wonderful, the kissing even better."

Tonight had been the best date of her life and just the thought of it made her smile. "Until we got caught. Thank you for stopping me. If you hadn't my father would have walked in on us and that is not exactly how I pictured my first time."

Squeezing her tightly, he laughed and then leaned back. "Your first time should be special. Not a rushed event on a sofa. A long, luxurious evening with champagne and chocolate and possibly a bubble bath together."

A blush spread across her cheekbones. "Mr. Lawrence, you still have that seductive spirit. That sounds like a splendid evening."

He grinned at her and gave her a quick peck on the lips. "Goodnight, Chloe."

"Goodnight," she said and watched him walk down the sidewalk to his car. The perfect ending to that conversation would be if he'd said *and that's what we'll do on our wedding night,* but right now, no promises had been made between them.

Turning to go into the house, she glanced back at the street. Her father must be blind, not to see Drew's expensive, red sports car parked in front of her house. So why was he here?

Walking back inside, her father sat sprawled where just a few minutes ago she and Drew were kissing.

"Drew seems to be changing into a nice man since he moved back."

Gazing at her father all comfy sitting on her sofa, she stared at him. "What's different? You didn't want me going out with Drew. Why the change of heart? The two of you seem to be great pals."

For a moment, she wasn't sure her father would answer her, his eyes narrowed.

"After watching the two of you at the church picnic, I went to Drew and asked him to marry you," he said softly.

Chloe felt her body go cold. She couldn't breathe as her lungs froze and she tensed. "Why the hell do you continue to interfere in my life? I'm sick of it, Dad. I'm a grown woman capable of finding my own dates and don't need your help."

So mad, she was shaking, she turned on her father but something in his expression halted her.

"You're right. But a father wants to make certain his daughter is taken care of before he dies." A long, heavy sigh escaped him sending a chill down her spine. Staring at her, his eyes filled with tears. "I've got pancreatic cancer and have about six months to live."

The floor tilted and she fell into a chair, tears burning her eyes, her throat tightly squeezed shut as the words reverberated in her head. Her father was dying.

❦

AT NINE O'CLOCK the next morning, Chloe went to Drew's office. Later today, he had a trial and she expected him to leave fairly early, but she needed to speak to him. All night she lay in bed awake, tossing and turning, crying one moment and furious the next. Because of her father, Drew decided to date her.

Not the Cupid statue. Not the superstition. Not the attraction between them, but her father.

When Drew unlocked the door to his rented office space, he

stared at her in surprise. She stood outside waiting. "Chloe? Is everything all right? Your father, is he ill?"

Pushing past him, she walked into the reception area. Tensing, she turned and glared at him. "How dare you connive with my father. I thought we were dating because you were genuinely interested in me. Not because my father asked you to go out with me."

Tears bubbled beneath the surface, but she continued. "How can I trust you if you would do something like this."

"Wait a minute," Drew said stepping toward her. "The only reason we're together is because I'm attracted to you. This has nothing to do with your father."

Could it be true or was he only saying this to get out of trouble?

"How am I suppose to believe that? After we ran the Cupid statue, you didn't want to go out with me. Didn't believe in this nonsense. So, when my father asks you to marry me, you suddenly decide now is the right time to ask me out? What kind of bribe did he offer you to date his poor daughter?"

Drew drug his hand through his hair. "No bribes and I told him I would go out with you with no guarantee of marriage."

"That's even worse."

"How? Did you want me to lie to the man?"

The night had been rough enough dealing with her father's illness, but she hoped this morning she would find clarity here with Drew. Hurt that Drew didn't start dating her until after her father requested he go out with her, but also enraged that he knew about her dad's cancer and never told her.

"No, but you can't commit to marriage. You obviously knew the truth about my father's health condition and you wasted what little time we have left for me to find someone to marry."

Drew tensed.

"If you had known he was dying, would you go out and find the first man just to make your father happy?" he asked. "All I asked was for some time to see where this connection took us. Woman, can't you see I'm so drawn to you? I can't sleep for dreaming of making love to you. You're the first woman I've dated seriously since high school. Give me a break."

That made her even madder. Now his lawyer logic kicked in and she needed to vent all the hurt feelings she'd been feeling since last night.

"According to the Cupid statue, we are each other's true loves."

"So, you think that because of a superstition, I should agree to marry you and live happily ever after? In my business, I witness the ugliness of marital bliss. Some days I wonder if there is such a thing as true love."

With a sarcastic nod, she didn't give him any slack. "Of course, you have, but would you ever marry me? Highly doubtful."

"You don't realize it, but I've committed more to you than any other woman. I need some time before I stand before your father and promise you forever. Is it wrong to want it to be right between us? All I'm asking for is time."

Again, lawyer logic when all she felt was despair. "My father doesn't have time. How could you keep his illness a secret from me?"

"I'm a man of my word and I promised him I wouldn't say anything. It was his duty to tell you, not me."

Cursing, Drew tried to reach out to her and she stepped back. "You agreed to date me while my father was ill, dying and wanted me married before he passed away. Yet you had no intentions of marrying me. You wasted my time and my father's precious time."

"Not true," he said.

Chloe paced the reception area, knowing there had to be a way to validate her point. And there was a way to find out his intent. One way for him to make her father happy. "Okay, prove it to me. Let's get married."

His eyes widened and she could see him looking like a

SYLVIA MCDANIEL

trapped animal. For a moment, he stared at her and her lungs froze, her breath sticking in her throat. "Exactly what I thought. You're wasting my time, Drew."

The door to his office cracked open and Anna Provinski walked out in her high heels, short mini dress, her makeup perfect. "Drew, honey, we need to leave."

Stuck in slow motion, her heart seemed to stop then start hammering in her chest. The crazy man was two timing her.

"Chloe, this is not what it looks like."

"Damn you, Drew." Turning, she all but ran for the door, furious that he never intended to marry her and now she had proof. Reforming Drew was just talk and nothing more. Drew Lawrence was still the same man whore and she'd become one of his victims.

Because she loved him.

CHAPTER 10

*D*rew glanced around at what Chloe created with his grandmother's old house and stared in amazement. She had taken his ideas and turned a sad older home into a comfortable, modern place that fitted his lifestyle and achieved his dreams. But somehow the happiness he expected in this home echoed empty.

A week had passed since she confronted him, put him on the spot and demanded he marry her. Sometimes he thought it would have been easier just to say I do. When did you know she was the one for you?

For years, women concocted everything imaginable trying to trap him into marriage. Leaving him with that hated feeling of being cornered.

Walking through the empty house, he came into his master bedroom and found a glass display case holding what appeared to be a diary.

Lifting the glass, he picked up the old leather-bound book, opened and recognized his mother's handwriting. Flipping to the last pages, his heart skipped a beat, and he froze as he comprehended the words.

Dear Diary,

Last night my friends persuaded me to try the Cupid dance... Coming to the end, a shiver of disbelief, scurried down his spine. His parents bumped into each other at the Cupid statue?

Engrossed in his mother's words, Drew sank to the floor to relived the tale of his parents' romance through her eyes.

Dear Diary,

James doesn't believe in the superstition or in getting married. After having dated half the high school graduating class, his intent is to remain single. Falling in love is too frightening for this big strong man and he would rather live alone.

So my plans are to continue on with my life and move to Fort Worth next week. I have a job and will be sharing an apartment with two other girls. Even though according to the legend, he's my true love, I'm done. I'm moving on with my life, and hopefully, eventually, I'll find someone else.

For the next thirty minutes, he continued reading the diary until he came to the end. Closing the book, he had no idea where Chloe found it, but what a special gift that touched his heart. The diary made him feel close to his mother once again. Helped him witness his father through her eyes and realize he was like his father.

Stubborn, resistant fool to love - who feared marriage and in the end, it brought him his life's greatest joy. Could that be what Drew was missing by not marrying Chloe?

His father fought saying *I do* until his mother finally walked away from her chance of love. It wasn't until later he understood what he lost and hunted her down, promising his love forever and telling her he was a damn fool for questioning their feelings.

Last week, Chloe had been emotional, almost to the point of irrational. Would things be different if he wrapped his arms around her and held her. First, she found out her father was dying and then Drew's part in her father's attempt at match-making and finally she came to a wrongful conclusion that he and Anna were sleeping together again. Why didn't he offer more support? Wouldn't that have soothed her and then they might have talked rationally?

Now, it was too late.

Drew loved Chloe, and like his father, was the biggest damn fool for doubting his emotions. Since she walked out, he'd learned first-hand the worst ache of loneliness. Sure, he'd been tempted to call up an old girlfriend to ease his pain, but he wanted Chloe, no one else. Indeed, he loved her and wanted to spend his life loving her.

Now that he realized he loved her, how could he prove his love enough to get her back?

DREW GLANCED up from the case he was working on to see his brothers walking into the house. Boxes were stacked everywhere as he only unpacked the bare necessities until his furniture arrived from his apartment in Dallas. So far, he loved living in a home filled with family history.

The only missing piece of his life was Chloe.

His brothers, Jim and Kyle walked in the door. "Drew," Jim said, looking around. "This is perfect. Chloe did a great job refurbishing this old house and making it look nice."

A beautiful house, an empty home without her there to share it with him, but he was trying his best to learn to adjust.

"How was the honeymoon?" Drew asked.

"You should try it sometime. Nothing like escaping for a few days to the mountains to relax and enjoy your wife. So, what's going on with you and Chloe? Haven't seen you two together lately."

Kyle sank down in a chair next to Drew. "Hey, brother, how's your love life?"

Leaning back Drew gazed at two most important men in his

life. "All right, what's up. Why do I feel like the love police have descended on my home and I'm about to be arrested for failing to yield?"

Jim looked at Kyle. "Sounds good to me. What do you think?"

"Convicted as charged. But I think he'll lawyer up before Ryan puts him behind bars."

The reason for this meeting was clear. Concern for a brother and they heard he and Chloe were no longer dating. The Cupid dance had lost.

"This feels familiar," Drew said. "Didn't I sit in on both of your 'come to the altar' meetings?"

"Is that what we're doing?" Jim inquired.

"Look, brother, we're happily married. Dancing around the God of Love I believed was a bunch of bunk, but somehow the outcome turned into happiness. What happened between you and your lady?"

What could Drew say without making it even worse. "Let's just say, I'm like our father. I'm just a nut case."

Jim frowned. "Our parents were not crazy."

"Well, I seem to have taken their traits and thrown in a dash of lunacy. Chloe made me realize that since Mom died, my sadness had me going out and sleeping with women, but never wanting a serious relationship.

"After we talked, I consulted a therapist and she gave it some fancy diagnosis and put me in a grief counseling group. Though Mom's been gone for years, it's helped me understand how to cope better with her loss."

His brothers stared at him like he had taken a nose dive over the edge of a cliff, but he didn't care. As a lawyer and a human being, he needed to understand his destructive behavior before it destroyed his life. Only his clients were the people he wanted to clean up after making terrible decisions.

When Chloe first mentioned his promiscuity could be linked to his mother's death, he thought it sounded ridiculous. Dr.

Goodman showed him how he searched for comfort in the form of a one-night stand.

Now the counseling group taught him how to handle her unexpected death. If he had known she would die that day, he would have been by her side, but it happened so suddenly.

"Wow, that is the last thing I expected to hear from you," Kyle said.

Promiscuous sex and the death of their parents didn't really go together and his brothers thought he was a playboy out having fun. The family never associated his actions with the over-whelming guilt and anguish of a loved one. How depression could cause you to act irresponsibly.

"So how does this make you similar to our parents?" Jim asked.

With an uncomfortable laugh, Drew began to tell their mother's tale. "While Chloe was demolishing the house, she must have found our mother's diary."

"Mom wondered where that book disappeared to," Jim said sitting up. "What does it say?"

Shaking his head, Drew smiled. "Did you know our father bumped into our mother running around the Cupid statue?"

Their eyes grew large as they stared at each other. "What? They never said anything. Why wouldn't they tell us," Kyle asked.

"Because Dad didn't want us kids to do anything outrageous like that silly Cupid superstition," Jim said. "I remember him telling me not to call him if I got caught dancing naked at that statue. He never said a word about him and Mom doing it."

"Why didn't she tell us?" Kyle said, throwing his hands up in the air. "Mom was always open with us."

"Mother promised him she would never tell any children they had about how they bumped into each other at the Cupid dance."

The brothers sat in silence for a moment. "When you're done, I want to read that diary," Jim said.

"Me, too," Kyle admitted. "Back to Drew. How does this affect you and your lady?"

Drew steepled his hands. "Our father resisted marrying our mother. She gave up on him and walked away determined to get over Dad, but at the eleventh hour, he came running back. We almost weren't born, gentleman."

"And you are resisting marrying Chloe," Jim asked.

"Yes," Drew said. "Yes, and to make things more complicated, her father's days are numbered and he would like to live long enough to see her marry."

For over a week, he had gone back and forth thinking of his options, deciding what he should do. Drew loved Chloe, but would she accept an engagement? Clarity came to him, and the answer before he asked the question.

Time to go all in or be kicked to the curb.

More than anything, this time alone had proven he loved Chloe. Even Anna, standing in front of him in her mini skirt and heels, told him he was a fool for not manning up and putting a ring on that girl's finger. At dinner, she said he needed to grow a set of balls, which not only shocked, but insulted him.

"What are you going to do?" Jim asked.

"Before you respond to that question. Do you love her?" Kyle asked.

"Madly," Drew said. "She's mad as hell at me and I can't blame her, but I'm going after her. I've been trying to think of a way that would prove to her I love her. It has to be something big, guys."

"Oh, we got this," Kyle said.

"Oh, yeah, we'll get you all fixed up."

CHLOE WAS WORKING on a new house. Redoing Drew's grandmother's house had gotten her two new clients and already she was in the demolition stage on one house. And it felt good to smash cabinets from the wall. The men in her crew stood way back when she swung the sledgehammer, putting all her body weight into knocking down walls.

With each blow, an exhilaration went through her.

"Chloe," she heard her foreman yell her name.

"What?" she asked really not wanting to be disturbed.

"Someone is here to see you," he said.

Whirling around, there stood Anna, Drew's girlfriend in the doorway. All work ceased as every eye stared at Anna's long legs, short skirt, and makeup fitting an actress.

"What do you want?" Right now, she didn't want to talk to the seductress who lured Drew away. The Devil take him, she could have him.

Liar, her heart immediately responded.

"A few minutes of your time, please," Anna said. "Outside where we can speak in private."

Dropping the hammer, everyone watched as she followed Anna out the door, wondering what the woman wanted.

When they stepped far enough away from the house, Anna stopped and turned to face her.

"Look, I realize you and Drew had been dating and somehow you think the two of us got re-entangled with each other, but that's not true. I'm a lawyer and Drew has been helping me on a divorce case in the next county over.

"Nothing romantically is happening between us and not from my lack of trying either. Girl, I don't know what you've done to that man, but he is steadfast in his devotion to you."

"The other morning you were in his office."

"Yes, we were on our way to Parker county courthouse to negotiate one of the largest divorce settlements in the state of Texas. That woman is now richer than God, thanks to our team-work," she said with a coo.

Chloe stood back, staring, considering what the woman was saying, not ready to admit everything was fine once again. Her world hadn't been right since the night her father told her of his illness.

"Whatever happened between the two of you devastated the man. Drew is suffering, and frankly, I think this mess is all one big misunderstanding. He needs you."

While it was good news, she still had questions.

"He's not been sleeping around again?"

Anna started laughing. "The man doesn't even glance at women anymore. At first, it was kind of sad, but now I understand the reason. I've always thought he needed to settle down some, but he turned off the tap water and hasn't gone in for a swim in a long time."

Chloe considered the woman for a moment. "You're not just covering for him."

Why would an ex-girlfriend cover for him, especially when she'd been trying to lure him back into her bed.

"Oh, honey, he doesn't have a clue I'm here and would probably be mad as hell if he found out. Whatever happened between the two of you was beautiful, but you need to bring it back and quick. He's meaner than a hornet's nest at an orgy."

A feeling of relief spread through Chloe. "Thank you for coming and telling me. Let's keep this our little secret. Let me think about it."

Anna reached out and hugged her. "For the sake of his clients, please make it hasty. You two are such a cute couple. You'll have beautiful babies."

"Before we start talking children, Drew and I need to see if there is a chance of us being a couple again."

CHAPTER 11

*A*fter church on Sunday, Chloe had planned on spending the afternoon doing laundry and relaxing. The last few weeks had been emotionally draining, and well, she needed some rest - a chance to recharge her batteries for the upcoming months.

She had also been spending a lot of time with her father. Needing to soak up as much of him as possible before he left her.

After lunch, her father said, "Let's take a stroll. I'd like to walk in the town square and then we can head home."

"Sounds nice," she said.

Placing her hand in the crook of his elbow, they walked along the tree-lined avenue.

"Sometimes parents get so wrapped up in their children, they forget to stop and think whether this is good for the child or not. Here, you are, a grown woman and I've been trying to find you a husband. You were right. It's none of my business. I'll do better at staying out of your affairs."

With a glance at her father, she smiled. "Agreed. But you also knew you were sick and you wanted to see me walk down the aisle. Unfortunately, I don't think that's going to happen."

SYLVIA MCDANIEL

"Oh, I'm still sending up prayers. I ask very little from God, so I think he could give this old man this last request. We'll just have to be patient and wait and see."

Chloe laughed. "Ever the optimist, Dad. Why aren't you praying for your recovery?"

"Maybe because I know my time is at hand and I'm okay with that."

A sigh escaped from Chloe. He thought it was his time, but she wasn't ready to let him go. So far, she had yet to find the time or the right words to say to Drew. The inspiration had not come to her.

The clatter of hooves sounded on the pavement and they both glanced up to see a beautiful white carriage - one that looked to belong in a Cinderella movie - coming toward them.

"Will you look at that," her father said.

A man in a black tuxedo handled the horses and another man sat in the back.

"Someone must be getting married today and this is their transportation to the wedding."

Her father laughed. "Maybe."

Suddenly the carriage halted right in front of them. Chloe's mouth fell open as she recognized Drew in the back wearing a white tuxedo. Funny, she'd seen him at church probably only an hour before. At that time, it seemed he avoided her and now here he was all dressed in white, top hat, tails, the complete outfit.

Oh my! A tremor of nerves went through her.

He stepped out of the vehicle and it was then she realized Jim, his brother, controlled the reins. She glanced up and down the street and saw his sister Kelsey, Shadow, and Tempe standing on the steps of the boutique watching. People from the congregation lined the sidewalks and she clasped her hand over her heart.

She turned to her father who stood by her side.

Drew moved to her father, a serious expression on his face. "Mr. Kilian, I know we spoke earlier, but I would like for you to

114

tell Chloe, that I came to you and asked for her hand in marriage. That you did not ask me to marry her, but I willingly came and told you I loved your daughter and would be honored if you would accept me into your family as her husband."

"Yes, son, you did. After we prayed, I gave you my blessing."

Shock shimmered through her as tears welled up in her eyes and her father slid into the background, leaving just the two of them.

Drew turned to Chloe. "We've had an unusual courtship. You've taught me a lot about myself. Because of you, I'm a changed man, a better man. Sometimes I'm a bit slow, but I love you, Chloe. I've loved you for weeks, months, in fact. I've been waiting for you to come into my life for years and then I almost screwed it up. There will never be anyone but you."

His hand got stuck in his pocket and finally he pulled out the box and knelt on one knee. "Will you marry me and make me the luckiest man in the world?"

Chloe couldn't believe her eyes. There in front of her was the man no one believed could be caught. There was her man, her love. "I just want to tell you, I've always known you were a great man. I love you, Drew. Yes, I'll marry you and love you for the rest of my days on earth."

Standing, he hauled her into his arms, while the crowd around them and lining the streets cheered. "I'm sorry, Drew, for not believing in you and for not giving you the time you needed. Everything came down on me at once and my time with my father was slipping away."

"Shhh...this is our happy moment. Our time to celebrate. Besides, after reading that diary you left me, you are correct. I'm my father's procrastinating son."

"And I'm my father's daughter. Love me till the end of time."

His lips came down on hers and he sealed their promise with a kiss.

❧

DREW COULDN'T BELIEVE how quickly everyone had come together for this wedding. His sister and sisters-in-law had each taken on part of the tasks and three weeks after he proposed to Chloe, they were getting married. Her father was getting his wish, Chloe was having her church wedding and Drew was marrying the woman of his dreams.

After his initial bout of nerves, he felt more confident than ever. No doubts remained about Chloe or their love.

The music started and he turned to his father-in-law who he'd grown to love.

"I'm putting my little girl in your care from this day forward. Treat her right."

"Yes, sir. I'll look after her."

"Mainly love her," her father said with a tear in his eye.

"Always," Drew promised.

"Come on, son, the bride is waiting."

Drew walked out the door and stood watching while her father went to the bride's room. A sense of peace overcame him as the scent of his mother's perfume filled the room. He realized her spirit looked down from heaven and probably even his father. Everyone they loved was here, including Chloe's mother. He didn't know how, but he knew and sensed their presence.

Chloe had insisted this be a family event and his sister and his brothers were all in the wedding party. Standing at the altar, he watched his brothers escort their wives down the aisle and Cody his sister. The day couldn't be any more special with his siblings standing up beside them as they took their vows.

The music grew louder and Chloe and her father started walking toward him. At the sight of his beautiful bride in her satin wedding dress and lacy veil, he feared his heart would explode from the love he had for this woman.

If someone told him he'd soon be happily wedded after

dancing naked around a Cupid statue, he would have laughed out loud at them. Now, he felt grateful to Cody and Kelsey for being the reason he was forced to do the Cupid Stupid dance.

And that group of church ladies who wanted to take the Cupid statue down would have a fight on their hands. Too many people, including his parents, had found love because of that piece of rock.

But the whole town thought no one would capture Drew's heart. No one but Chloe. Only the preacher's daughter had faith and tamed the bad boy. Tonight, for the first time, he would make her his and he could hardly wait to show her how much he loved her.

Kissing her on the cheek, her father placed her hand in his and she smiled, her eyes brimming with love. Their first night together, he hoped and prayed they made a child, so her father would hopefully live long enough to see his grandchild. More than anything, he looked forward to sharing his love with her and claiming his bride.

Her father cleared his throat. "Bow your heads and pray for God's blessing on this couple."

And now their life together began.

AND NOW...CUPID Santa

Brie Simpson glanced around the town square at the granite boy in a diaper with his bow drawn back, arrow ready to strike. What was a practical, logical woman like herself doing standing naked in a park waiting for the clock to strike the dancing hour? Never one for crazy stunts, she feared if seized by the law, her friends and family would assume she finally went off the deep end.

Her luck with men was like a bad hand of craps in Vegas. Lucky seven appeared at the wrong time. Sure, dancing in the buff to find happily ever after was a superstition. One that could find her looking out between bars.

The numbers of couples who admitted to having met because of the Cupid Stupid run proved something about this dance brought people together. Enough people, that here she stood in her birthday suit, hoping the man she encountered would accept her plus-size body.

The clanging gong struck midnight, the ding dong resounding throughout the city. Her stomach clenched as excitement spiraled its way through her, and yet, she didn't know if that was anticipation or cold. Ready to get this process started, she began to jog, shivering in the cold as she chanted the words the tradition required. "Oh Cupid, find me my true love. Oh Cupid, find me my true love."

According to the legend, at least three laps around the God of Love were mandatory, more if you were desperate. At the ripe old age of thirty, even the sixty-year-old janitor in her building looked appealing. Eager to marry and have the family she dreamed of, she was willing to risk it all tonight.

On the third lap, she spotted a figure coming around the statue and sped up.

"Stop," he called. "Halt."

Taking a glance behind her, Santa ran toward her, chasing her and she busted out laughing.

"Freeze, I'm the law."

"Law? Where's your badge and gun?"

The jolly old man huffed and puffed. Seemed Santa skipped the gym lately.

"Deputy Stephen Austin of Cupid."

The father of Texas? Dressed like Santa Claus claiming to be an officer?

"And I'm Pocahontas. Leave me alone. I'm finding true..."

Stunned, she stopped, staring at the man running, her chest

seizing as she stared at Santa Claus. "Oh my, you're my true love. But you're old."

As he ran up to her, he slapped the handcuffs around her wrist sending a trickle of fear up her spine.

"I'm your worst nightmare. You're under arrest for public indecency," he said.

Available at All Retailers!

Thank You For Reading!

Dear Reader,

Oh my goodness, this book was one of the most difficult to write in the series. Why? I loved the hero, but I wanted you, the reader to like him. This couple quickly became one of my favorite couples. Hope you enjoyed them.

As always, if you're inclined, please go to your favorite retailer and let others know what you think. Whether or not you loved the book or hated, it-I'd enjoy your feedback.

Sign up for my newsletter if you'd like to learn about my new releases before everyone else. Join the readers group on Facebook. Thanks for venturing into my world and I hope to see you here again soon.. And remember, I do not condone dancing naked around a Cupid statue!!

Sincerely,

Sylvia McDaniel

www.SylviaMcDaniel.com
Sylvia@SylviaMcDaniel.com

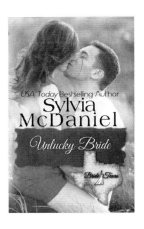

The Unlucky Bride

Flood waters and broken hearts…two jilted ex-lovers trapped in Bride, Texas

Laney Baxter's ironic escape to Bride, Texas couldn't be more fitting - considering she is a runaway bride! Unfortunately, her plans to hide out have her jumping from the frying pan into the fire when she discovers she is trapped with the one man who broke her heart years ago - Chase Hamilton! Now, she can only hope the rising waters recede before Chase uncovers the mystery of their past.

Chase returns to Bride, Texas to nurse a broken heart and re-evaluate his life. The family home along the river was supposed to offer him peace and quiet, not the last woman he ever expected to see again. When the river rises, trapping them together, Chase questions whether his heart was really broken or just his ego bruised.

Laney and Chase are forced to face some startling revelations -

including the feelings they still have for each other. Can the two work through their tangled emotions before the river recedes, or will long hidden secrets tear them apart?

Available at All Retailers!

Chapter One

Cupid, Texas

"Valentine's Day. Today is the cheating snake's wedding day," Taylor Braxton said, flipping her blonde hair over her shoulder before taking a sip of wine. Her third glass of the evening. "I'd like to propose a toast to his new wife. May she never find him in her bed with someone else, like I found her in mine."

The three women clinked glasses.

"Maybe it was for the best. After all, lawmen are known for being serial cheaters," Meghan, one of Taylor's best friends, said in her quiet librarian voice. She gave a shake of auburn hair, her emerald eyes filled with sympathy.

Still the same after all these years, Taylor wondered if Meghan ever raised her voice even during a climax. Did she scream with passion, or just say oh? And Taylor never wanted to know the answer to that question.

Yes, lawmen cheated, but many men were sleazebags who thought infidelity was nothing.

Kelsey, Taylor's other best friend leaned in close. "Well, if you hadn't found him locked in the arms of another woman, you wouldn't have come back to Cupid."

"True," Taylor agreed.

Pushing her dark brunette hair back over her shoulder, Kelsey smiled. "I can't believe we're all here together again. Just like the old days when we were young and naive and so vulnerable. Now, we're all grown up and--"

"Still single," Meghan said with a sigh.

"Yep, no eligible man on my radar," Kelsey admitted. "Who would want to date a woman with three pain in the ass brothers watching over her?"

Kelsey's announcement surprised Taylor. Of the three of them, Kelsey was who she thought would walk down the aisle first. Instead, not one of them was wearing a ring, and frankly, she found it odd she'd come the closest to a honeymoon.

"I don't want a man. I'm giving up. I'm going to remain single the rest of my life," Taylor announced.

After her last attempt at love, the time to step away had arrived in the form of a revealed booty call. Now, her focus on the family business was the most important thing in her life.

"Oh yeah, that's the life I want," Meghan replied, sarcasm dripping in her tone. "Always the third wheel when you're around couples. Every holiday your relatives asking if there is something wrong with you or have you tried online dating. Blind dates with your next-door neighbor's son, who is so kind that he still lives with his mother." She shivered. "No, thanks."

Meghan's appearance fitted the sweet, innocent librarian image, but her tongue was sharp and precise. Sometimes even Taylor was shocked at what came out of her smart mouth.

Setting her wine glass down on the table Kelsey leaned forward. "Or your brothers' glancing at every man you bring home like he's a terrorist, and should they learn he's sleeping with their sister, he would wake up six feet under." Kelsey giggled. "They don't know, but I lost my virginity the first semester of college during pledge week."

"Ohh...with someone you cared about?" Taylor asked.

She sighed. "Not really. We were two virgins who wanted to rid ourselves of the stigma. A fumbling, truly awful, awkward experience. After that horrible first time, I concentrated on my studies and not on men."

"What about you, Taylor? When did you lose your virginity?" Meghan asked.

"Prom night," she said, shaking her head. "Billy Ray Smith."

"Oh my gosh, he's married and living one town over."

"Thank God. He was mistake number one. I was young and foolish." And oh, so stupid, she thought.

That night he'd convinced her everyone was doing the nasty and if she didn't give it up, she would be the only virgin left in school. Curious about the forbidden fruit and wanting to fit in, she listened to him.

Meghan laughed. "Well, we certainly know who popped my cherry. Max Vandenberg, football superstar jerk."

The three women sighed. Kelsey shifted uneasily in her chair. "We thought we were going to change the world."

Taylor snickered. "I think the world changed us."

Meghan giggled. "Remember that silly superstition from high school?"

"Which one? There were several," Kelsey said. "I especially liked the one where the football boys had to put a pair of girl's panties on the top of the goal post if they wanted a winning season."

So many things happened in a small town where gridiron was king. The football team could get away with so much more than the other school sports.

"While the drill team practiced in our uniforms, all our undies were stolen from the girls' gym. I remember going commando, like, yesterday." Taylor chuckled.

Kelsey turned toward her. "Max Vandenberg was the panty thief. Did you hear that he played professional football for the Dallas Cowboys for a while?"

"Until he got hurt. Now he's back." Meghan shook her head. "Right back here under my nose - the big jerk. He's coaching at my school."

"Why does it seem like many of our classmates left and eventually returned."

"Yes, Ryan Jones is back. My brother told me he's sheriff now," Kelsey said, drinking another glass of vino. "He was my ex. So two exes back in town and another one's married and lives nearby."

"I don't consider Billy Ray an ex."

Sure, Taylor lost her virginity the night of prom, but recognized she would never marry Billy Ray. *Redneck* was a polite term for that kid. The ex that crushed her was in Dallas where he belonged with his skanky new wife.

Sitting there, she glanced at her besties from grade school.

"Wonder how many girls fell for that Cupid superstition? Did you guys ever do that one?" Taylor asked.

"Oh no," Meghan said. "I didn't like getting undressed in gym class."

"Oh no," Kelsey echoed. "If my brothers caught me dancing naked around the statue in the town square, I would have been sealed away in a nunnery until my female parts shriveled. What about you?"

"No," she said, thinking she didn't believe that nonsense.

Taylor looked at the two women sitting at the table. She poured the last of the second bottle of wine. The music seemed louder, the laughter shriller, and yet she was having so much fun, she didn't want to stop. Tomorrow she'd probably regret the amount of alcohol they were consuming, but tonight felt good. Old friends, memories, and alcohol helping her forget the importance of this damn day.

"You remember when all the cheerleaders did the naked Cupid dance, all hoping to find their true love. How did the magic work out for them?" Kelsey said with a laugh.

Taylor shook her head. "I remember. The football team showed up unexpectedly with cameras in hand and when the squad returned to school they faced suspension."

The principal had decided to make them examples.

Meghan frowned and gazed at the women, her blue eyes large, her expression one of disgust. "Don't feel too badly for them. They're all married. In fact, most of them have babies. If the superstition is true, it worked very well for them. What the hell is wrong with us?"

Taylor threw her hands up. "I'm not looking to get married. Right now, my focus is my parents' restaurant. I don't need a man."

After her disastrous engagement, the time had come to put the idea of marriage and children and happily ever after on the shelf.

Turning in her chair, Meghan looked at Kelsey. "What about you? Do you want to marry?"

Kelsey leaned on her hands. "Yes, I would like to find a man, but my brothers run them off faster than a deer during hunting season. So I'll be working on the boutique I'm preparing to open for business. One year is all I have to make a profit. Or I'll be moving back to the city. What about you, Meghan?"

She tossed back her hair and stared them straight in the eye. "I'm twenty-five years old. I'm ready. My ovaries are beginning to shrivel like a prune. Bring on the right man and I'll race him to the altar."

The idea hit Taylor smack in the stomach, and while it seemed preposterous, the idea was too good to pass up. She shook her head at the two of them, giggling. "Then let's do it."

Frowns appeared on their faces as they stared at her. "What?"

She checked her watch. "It worked for all those other women. Why not us? The superstition says at midnight anyone chanting and dancing naked around the fountain will soon meet their true love. I've never believed in the notion, but hey, I'm game. We've got thirty minutes. Let's go kick some Cupid butt and see if that superstition is real or not."

Meghan's eyes widened. "You want me to take off my clothes and dance in front of you and everyone else in town, chanting some silly verse?"

"Oh, most people will be asleep and I've seen you *au naturel* before. I'll be too busy dancing to notice you and your jiggling tatas."

Laughing, Kelsey gazed at Taylor. "And you think this is going to work."

No, she didn't believe in superstitions. She walked under ladders, stepped on cracks, and black cats didn't frighten her. Friday the thirteenth was just another day and dancing without clothes around a statue wasn't going to land her a husband.

She didn't want or need a man in her life. But she'd do this for her friends.

"We're late bloomers. Everyone else did this in high school. We never had the courage, but now we're older, some of us desperate. Let's do it."

Kelsey lifted her glass and drained the alcohol. "I'm in. What about you, Meghan?"

"Oh, it's starting again. During high school, you girls could get me into more trouble. You're back in town less than twenty-four hours and already you're plotting mischief."

"Oh, come on, it'll be fun," Taylor said, downing the last of her drink and signaling the waitress.

"The temperature outside is colder than a well digger...and we're getting naked," Meghan whined. "Tonight, other women are being wined and dined and we're going to dance without our clothes, in the town square? Something is wrong with this picture."

"Think of the thrill. The tales you can tell your children," Taylor said, the adventure of doing something dangerous sending a ripple of excitement through her. Years had passed since her last prank and this was the kind of stunt that got her juices flowing.

"Daring." Kelsey grabbed her purse. "I haven't done anything like this since college. I'm just drunk enough my logical, rational side is being held hostage by my fun side."

"Are you in?" Taylor asked not certain Meghan would agree.

With a sigh Meghan finished her wine. "I don't want to be the only old maid. Of course, I'm in."

Taylor was giggling hard when they left the bar, the three of them laughing as they all but dragged poor Meghan. The girl was always a laggard, but give her enough alcohol and she knew how to party with the best of them. At least, she had years ago. They hadn't been bad kids, just teenagers testing their new adult skills and failing more often than not.

"I could be fired if we're caught," Meghan said. "Public nudity is not exactly the proper behavior for the school librarian. My contract says something about a moral issue."

Moral, schmoral - they weren't holding an orgy. A little silly fun that had gotten many kids in trouble.

Kelsey handed her the bottle of wine they'd managed to sneak out of the bar. "Take a swig, Meghan, it will give your courage a boost. Besides, we're not going to get caught. We're not stupid teenagers."

"No, we're stupid adults," Taylor said smiling. College was the last time she'd done anything this wild and crazy. Her sorority had broken into Phi Beta Kappa's house and stolen all the jock straps, greased them with Vaseline, and hung the undergarments in the trees outside the gym.

Clouds drifted across the moon casting eerie shadows and she felt a rush of excitement. "Five minutes until midnight. Hurry, girls."

Squealing, they ran the final two blocks to the fountain. They arrived, huffing and puffing, and stopped to stare at the sculptured God of Love.

"Dancing around this statue is going to help us find the man of our dreams?" Kelsey questioned. "Whoever made up this shit is sitting back somewhere laughing at how many fools stripped off their clothes and danced in the moonlight."

"In the middle of freaking winter," Meghan added.

Part of Taylor agreed with Kelsey, but the other part, the more reckless and wild part, urged her on. "Come on, girls, we're doing this. We're going to prove this is either the biggest farce in town, or it's going to work for my friends. Just not for me."

"I hope this is worth it," Meghan said as they all began to remove clothing, each one looking to make certain they weren't the only one stripping.

"Will it look funny if I leave my boots on?" Kelsey asked.

"Naked. You have to be naked according to the superstition," Taylor said, yanking off her footwear, the cold stones hard against her feet.

"As soon as the church bell strikes midnight, we're going to dance around the statue for one minute. Then I'm putting my clothes on and walking home," Meghan said, shivering in the buff. "You girls are going to be the death of me yet. If I come down sick--"

"We'll have a hot looking guy deliver you a box of Kleenex and chicken soup."

Kelsey started laughing. "Look, girls, I got a boob job while I was in college. Aren't they nice?"

She held up her tits for all to see and Meghan turned away groaning. "What am I doing?"

"I'm not looking at your breasts," Taylor said, giggling as she removed her bra. Maybe this wasn't one of her smarter ideas. The cold had her own poor nipples shriveled to the size of a raisin.

"Hurry, midnight is almost here," Meghan said, her words slurred from the alcohol. "Let's do this and put our clothes back on before we catch pneumonia."

"We better get some action from this," Kelsey replied, jumping up and down on the sidewalk, nude.

"And not legal action," Taylor said with a giggle.

After she finished undressing, she folded her jeans and sweater neatly and placed them on a bench. "Okay, I'm ready. Let's do this."

Passing the bottle of wine one more time, laughing and chuckling and hoping the alcohol would give them some much needed warmth, Taylor tried not to look down.

"We're being so naughty," Meghan said, giggling drunkenly. "Never again."

"Oh, come on, next week we're taking you skinny dipping at the lake," Kelsey said.

"Not during the winter, we're not," Taylor replied.

The church bells started to chime. With a scream, they laughed and began to run and dance, giggling hysterically as the three of them ran around the God of love.

"Oh, Cupid statue find us our true love," they chanted as they danced nude around the fountain in the town square, laughing at the absurdness of what they were doing.

"Nuts," Meghan said. "All this is going to do is give us frostbite on our girly bits."

Taylor thought she might be right, but what a way to go. It felt freeing and exhilarating and she couldn't think of a single crazy thing that could pique this outing.

Headlights turned onto the street and they glanced at each other, their eyes wide. Shrieking, their hands trying to cover their female parts, they ran but their clothes were too far away.

"Oh no," Meghan said.

Red beacons flashed on top of the car. A shiver of fear raced down Taylor's spine setting panic into motion.

"Run, girls," Taylor yelled. "Run, it's the sheriff. Everyone split up, he can't arrest us all."

Kelsey and Meghan ran in different directions, running down the intersecting streets, leaving their clothes and purses behind.

Taylor wasn't departing without her boots. The footwear had set her back almost a month's pay and she couldn't leave them on a park bench. Grabbing her stuff, she tried to pick up her friends' as well, but her arms were full.

Lights shined on her.

"Halt," a man's voice instructed. "Drop everything."

Oh great, she was the one who would be going to jail for dancing in her birthday suit in the public square.

჻

During football season, Sheriff Ryan Jones caught one or two young teenage girls either about to dance or dancing naked around the Cupid statue. He kept encouraging the council to remove the statue, but tonight, three grown women with well developed female bodies were doing the Cupid Stupid move. Long legs, perfect round asses, and breasts that were mouthwatering tempting.

Sworn to protect and serve, he pushed the images from his brain and told his cock to go back to sleep. False emergency.

Valentine's Day, he'd meant to be here earlier before the bells dinged midnight, but the Raffsberger's cat created a disturbance in the alley that sent him on a feline pursuit. That pussy caused him more trouble than even the town drunk, Simon Connally. At least he could lock up Simon, but the feline stared at him with those laughing green eyes. Once again, the sheriff was on a cat chase.

Missing midnight, he'd arrived just in time to find three nude women dancing and chanting around the God of Love. And one of them was none other than Taylor Braxton. A girl from high

134

school who if he hadn't been dating her best friend, he would have chased. But that was years ago.

"Don't move," he yelled, jumping out of his car and walking toward her. He didn't pull out his gun, because frankly, he didn't think she qualified as a dangerous criminal.

"Hi, Sheriff," she said, chattering and shivering in the cold, her arms crossed over her breasts, a palm covering her womanly bits. "How are you tonight?"

"I'm warmer than you," he replied, unable to stop his eyes from taking advantage of her nakedness. "Aren't you a little old for this?"

Jumping up and down, her arms wrapped across her breasts as she tried to get warm, he admired her curves. Since he'd been her best-friend's boyfriend right up until graduation, he never had a chance to pursue her before leaving for the military. And it was just as well given how Kelsey let everyone know her feelings about him when they broke up.

"Desperate times call for desperate measures," Taylor said, her teeth clicking as she shivered.

"Oh, you're desperate to find love?" Maybe it was his lucky night after all.

"No, but my friends think they're sitting on the shelf. I don't need a man."

Oh crap, he didn't like the sound of this conversation, and during his time in the Marines, those words were repeated to him more times than he cared to admit.

He laughed. "One of those."

"What do you mean one of those?" she asked, her voice rising. "Don't you think you could let me put my clothes on?"

He ignored her statement. One of the consequences of her Cupid Stupid dance was what he called his law enforcement embarrassment. Sometimes in order to keep people from doing a silly thing more than once, you let them experience the effects of their actions. "A woman who is anti-men."

She shrugged. "Maybe. Maybe I have reason to be."

Walking behind her, he took out his cuffs. "Place your hands behind your back."

"Oh, come on, Ryan, you know I'm not dangerous."

Sure, he knew she wasn't threatening, but she needed to be taught a scary lesson.

"You're breaking the law," he said, leaning in close. A whiff of her breath let him know she'd consumed alcohol. "I'd say you're intoxicated and naked and both of those are against the law."

"We had a little too much fun."

"Come on, uncross your arms and put them behind your back," he said, feeling like he was being mean, but making an example of her so her girlfriends wouldn't be tempted to try again.

Moving her arms to the back, he almost regretted her compliance. She had a nice set of breasts that made his job even more difficult.

"Your girlfriends ran off and left you to face the consequences of your actions," he responded, slipping the cuffs around her wrists.

"Look, we were celebrating my ex getting married on Valentine's Day. We drank too much wine and decided we never did this in high school. We'd do it now."

A twinge of sympathy gripped his stomach. Okay, perhaps she had a reason to be drinking.

"I ruined the party," he said, glancing around the park, knowing they were long gone or just waiting for the opportunity to claim their clothes. "Where did your friends take off to? They're also under arrest."

"Oh no," Taylor said. "I'm not talking. I'm not giving up any information on them."

Strolling to the bench, he observed all the clothing. "They left their purses and clothes behind."

She cursed. Opening the first handbag, he pulled out the

driver's license. "Meghan Scott. Isn't she the new school librarian? The school board will be displeased to hear she's got a warrant out."

He remembered the cute little auburn spitfire from school. She'd seemed so sweet and innocent and seeing her naked butt running down the street was quite pleasant.

"Please, Ryan, she didn't want to do this and I convinced her. She'll be fired."

"I can tell you who the third person is without even opening her purse. Kelsey Lawrence."

Taking the heap of clothing to his car, he grabbed a blanket from the backseat and carried it back to her. He didn't want to take her to jail. The paperwork, the embarrassment for her, the scarring of her permanent record. It was what he called the Stupid Cupid prank. Over the last two years, he'd seen it dozens of times.

Wrapping the woolen cloth around her, she lifted her chin defiantly and met his gaze. "You're really going to take me to jail?"

Not responding, he led her to his car and eased her into the back, like a common thief. She sighed, the sound dejected.

"I never thought I would have to call someone to bail me out."

"No, you never thought you would get caught dancing naked in the middle of town," he said, shutting the back door of his patrol car.

Crawling into the driver's seat he looked in the rearview mirror. "Where do you live?"

She frowned. "Nine twenty-six Hideaway Court. Why?"

He started the car and drove, letting her think he was taking her in. "Do you think your girlfriends are close by?"

"Don't have a clue. But you have their clothes. So I'm sure they're out of sight somewhere."

Chuckling, he drove to her townhouse only a couple blocks from downtown. "What did you do with your car?"

"I walked to the club. Due to the nature of our celebration, I thought it would be best to walk in case I had too much to drink. I didn't want to get a DUI or hurt someone."

Pulling in front of her house, she was quiet as he parked. Silence filled the automobile, even his radio had stopped crackling. Why did he feel like the boy in the diaper delivered him some good fortune? How did he go about asking a naked woman in the back seat of his patrol car for a date without looking like a real perv? He didn't.

"Every year, I arrest or take home kids who have decided to test the Cupid Stupid superstition. Seldom do I detain grownups, but if I do, I take them to the pokey where they belong. You're receiving a break for several reasons. One, you didn't drink and drive, and two, you said your ex was married today. For those two reasons, I'm giving you a pass. If I ever catch you near that damn sculpture, nude again, you will be charged and incarcerated."

Over the last year, he'd taken ten naked dumb kids home to their parents and only arrested one adult. And the reason the man had woken up incarcerated was because he'd been inebriated and waving his dick around peeing on the figure. City workers had to scrub the statue and drain the fountain while Ryan tried to convince the city council to knock down the God of Love.

"Thank you," she said, relief evident in her voice. "Are you going to press charges against my friends?"

"No, but you give them my warning. Any of you girls ever do this stunt again, I'll be waiting."

Usually his threat was enough to make people regret their decision.

"I'll remove the handcuffs and help you carry their stuff inside." He crawled out of the car.

Going to the back, he opened the door. "Lean forward."

As he unlocked the cuffs, his eyes feasted on her lovely rounded derrière.

"You know, I've never been cuffed before, and I must say they're very uncomfortable."

"They're supposed to be," he said and released her.

Pulling her arms in front of her she rubbed her wrists, keeping the blanket firmly tucked around her. Reaching for her hand, he helped her from the car. She stood and they were face to face, staring at each other, and he had the craziest urge to kiss her. Her lips were so ripe and full that he wanted to pluck them with his own. That craving would have to wait for another night.

"Thanks again, Ryan. I know what we did was crazy, but we didn't plan on getting caught."

"Nobody ever does. They think they're going to get away with the silly antic."

She stepped out of the way and he reached in and pulled out the stack of jeans, boots, and purses. "I'll drive around and see if I can find Meghan and Kelsey."

"They won't come out for you."

"It was nice of you to take the fall for them," he said, thinking not many women would do that for their friends.

"I persuaded them we should do this. I'm the one at fault."

"Yet, you don't want to marry?" he asked, shaking his head. "Seems kind of crazy."

"We did it for fun. Meghan wants to get married, but I barely escaped the noose once. I'm not looking for another chance," she said.

All he could think was, too bad. He'd been drawn to her in high school and now a mature woman, she was even better.

Hurrying to her door, she dug in her handbag for her key, the blanket sliding down, exposing her shoulder. Once the portal opened, a red dachshund greeted them, barking and yelping his happiness at her being home, the dog's nails sticking in the blanket and edging it down.

"Zeus, down," she commanded.

Ryan followed behind her, carrying in the stack of clothes and boots. Boxes sat on the floor. The townhouse had a homey atmosphere, but clearly she'd just moved back into town.

Turning to face him with the cloth tucked carefully around her hiding all her girly parts, she gazed at him. "Why don't you come by the restaurant one day and I'll fix something special for you. Not one of the regular items, but a specialty I'm working on not on the menu yet."

Now was not the time to ask her out; he knew dinner would be the perfect moment to ask.

"I'll come by tomorrow," he said.

"I'll have chicken picante waiting for you."

"Looking forward to it."

"Goodnight, Officer Ryan," she said and walked him to the door, shutting it behind him.

Stepping out onto the porch, he glanced up at the stars shining brightly. In Afghanistan, the nighttime stars had been brilliant, almost like he could reach out and touch them. A trickle of unease scurried down his spine and he pushed the memories away.

Maybe coming back to Cupid had been a good idea after all. Taylor Braxton had become a hot looking woman. All he had to do was convince her to go out with him. And he would, tomorrow.

Available Free at all Retailers!

Kyle Lawrence must fulfill a bet by dancing naked around the Cupid statue at midnight. Only he doesn't believe in the superstition of finding true love, and at this moment, he doesn't have time for forever after. A beautiful investigator from the USDA has arrived to warn of a possible cattle epidemic.

Life has not been easy for Dr. Tempest Tangier. A no nonsense veterinarian, who arrives in Cupid to investigate the possibility of a deadly cattle disease and end the infectious spread. But when she shows up at the Lawrence clinic, only to see a naked man breaking in, she quickly realizes the town holds more secrets than her past.

Can a rigid doctor with a famous past and a veterinarian with a gentle heart determined to save the cattle and the livelihood of his neighbors work together and in the process rescue each other?

Available at All Retailers!

Contemporary Romance
Return to Cupid, Texas
Cupid Stupid
Cupid Scores
Cupid's Dance
Cupid Help Me!
Cupid Cures
Cupid's Heart
Cupid Santa
Cupid Second Chance
Return to Cupid Box Set Books 1-3

Contemporary Romance
My Sister's Boyfriend
The Wanted Bride
The Reluctant Santa
The Relationship Coach
Secrets, Lies, & Online Dating

Bride, Texas Multi-Author Series
The Unlucky Bride

The Langley Legacy
Collin's Challenge

Short Sexy Reads
Racy Reunions Series
Paying For the Past
Her Christmas Lie
Cupid's Revenge
Science/Fiction Paranormal
The Magic Mirror Series
Touch of Decadence

Touch of Deceit

Also By Sylvia McDaniel

Western Historicals
A Hero's Heart
Ace's Bride
Second Chance Cowboy
Ethan

American Brides
Katie: Bride of Virginia

The Burnett Brides Series
The Rancher Takes A Bride
The Outlaw Takes A Bride
The Marshal Takes A Bride
The Christmas Bride
Boxed Set

Lipstick and Lead Series
Desperate
Deadly
Dangerous
Daring
Determined
Deceived

Scandalous Suffragettes of the West
Abigail
Bella
Callie – Coming Soon
Faith
Mistletoe Scandal

Southern Historical Romance
A Scarlet Bride

The Cuvier Women
Wronged
Betrayed
Beguiled
Boxed Set

Want to learn about my new releases before anyone else? Sign up for my New Book Alert and receive a free book.

USA Today Best-selling author, Sylvia McDaniel is an award-winning author of over thirty western historical romance and contemporary romance novels. Known for her sweet, funny, family-oriented romances, Sylvia is the author of The Burnett Brides a historical western series, The Cuvier Widows, a Louisiana historical series, Lipstick and Lead, a western historical series and several short contemporary romances.

Former President of the Dallas Area Romance Authors, a member of the Romance Writers of America®, and a member of Novelists Inc, her novel, A Hero's Heart was a 1996 Golden Heart Finalist. Several other books have placed or won in the San Antonio Romance Authors Contest, LERA Contest, and she was a Golden Network Finalist.

Married for over twenty years to her best friend, they have two dachshunds and a good-looking, grown son who thinks there's no place like home. She loves gardening, hiking, shopping, knitting and football (Cowboys and Bronco's fan).

www.SylviaMcDaniel.com
The End!

Made in United States
North Haven, CT
18 October 2021

10399919R10087